SEA

This is the story of Josh and Rocky, two young teens from entirely different worlds, who collide in the heat of a New York summer. A naïve boy from California, Josh comes to New York to visit his Uncle Jake, a sentimental elder whose eccentricities are only exceeded by his warmth and passion for life. Rocky is the beautiful daughter of a rabbi from Brooklyn, whose one dying wish is to understand what it means to be a complete woman before she runs out of time. With seemingly little in common, the two young friends quickly find that they are incomplete without each other and that the span of a brief summer is all the time they may ever have. It is with this realization in mind that they are able to embrace hope in the face of a tragedy few relationships could endure.

SEASON OF FAITH

Praise For Lawrence Kelter

"Lawrence Kelter is an exciting new novelist, who reminds me of an early Robert Ludlum." —Nelson DeMille

"Kelter is a master, pure and simple." —The Kindle Book Review

"Irresistible; a contemporary tour de force!" —James Siegel, NY Times Best-selling Author

SEASON OF FAITH

LAWRENCE KELTER

SEASON OF FAITH

Lawrence Kelter

SEASON OF FAITH

Lawrence Kelter

This book is a work of fiction. Names, places, characters, and incidents are the product of the author's imagination or are used fictitiously. Any resemblance to events, locales, or persons living or dead, is coincidental.

First Edition – April 2012

ISBN-13: 978-1470078027 ISBN-10: 1470078023

AUTHOR'S NOTE: A brief glossary of Yiddish terms can be found following the last page of this story.

For
Jenny and Ollie

Acknowledgments

The author gratefully acknowledges the following special people for their contributions to this book.

For my wife, Isabella, for her love, support, and tireless dedication to the perfection of this book.

For my children, Dawn and Chris, for making me smile.

SEASON OF FAITH

Lawrence Kelter

CHAPTER ONE

I will never forget the summer of 1969. I vacationed with my Uncle Jake in Brooklyn that year, and a dying girl taught me what it meant to be a man.

We lived in Beverly Hills. My father never said we were rich, but I knew we were. He used to say we were well off, but I came to understand that well off and wealthy were one and the same thing.

If you lived in Beverly Hills, the "in" thing that year was to take a European vacation without the kids, and my parents were ever so determined to keep up with the Joneses. My mom and dad had been planning it for months. They talked about it day and night, where to go, what to eat, how to pack, and so on and so on and so on.

I could tell that they felt guilty about sending me off to Uncle Jake's for the summer, even though he had been out to visit us a few times and they knew that I liked him a lot. They would ask me if it was okay about five times every day. The truth is, I was glad to go. My dad had told me a million great stories about Brooklyn. He had grown up there and was always talking fondly about the good old days. From the way he spoke, Brooklyn sounded like some kind of magical place where incredible things happened. I wanted to see Brooklyn for myself—this special place where the good old days had taken place. I wanted to experience some magic for myself.

I had become pretty tired of hearing my dad mangle the French language. He had no command of it, which was surprising for such a successful businessman, a big shot Hollywood producer for crying out loud. *"Croy-sense, croy-sense, croy-sense"* . . . the word was *croissant, pronounced kwa-san*, but he just couldn't hear the difference. He would ask for one every time we went out for breakfast. I can't tell you how many times I wished he would just give up and order a buttered roll. And my mother, *God*, she was becoming so horribly European, always talking on the phone with her friends about Chanel this and Dior that. It was getting to be too much.

All of the tour books mentioned that travelers were wise to bring along a roll of toilet paper, as European hotels did not always have adequate supplies on hand. For some reason, the fact that she had to pack her own TP for the trip didn't seem to bother her. For Pete's sake, I was sure even Uncle Jake had toilet paper. No toilet paper, really?

On the seventh of July 1969, I awoke in Uncle Jake's bedroom, having arrived from Los Angeles the night before. It had been a long trip, and I slept until almost 11:00 a.m. Mom always said that I was a good sleeper.

The window air conditioner that had been humming when I went to bed was now conspicuously quiet. The room was filled with hot, stagnant air. The first thing I noticed was that the room smelled a little bit like Uncle Jake. Heat and humidity had combined to drive his aroma from the closet, the chest of drawers, and the bedding. Let's just say that it wasn't the bouquet of California orange blossoms I was used to. My suitcase was open on the floor alongside the bed. I reached into it, grabbed my Brut cologne pump, and began deodorizing. It wasn't exactly the scent of orange blossoms, but it wasn't as stinky as a seventy-year-old's decrepit underpants either.

I really wasn't one of those spoiled, rich brats. I would have slept in the spare bedroom, but Uncle Jake insisted that it was too small and that I'd be more comfortable in his bedroom. I had been too tired to argue with him after the long flight. I was not quite thirteen, and well, Uncle Jake was seventy, so I didn't think I stood a chance in a debate with him. Sometimes you just have to smile and say yes. I later learned that Uncle Jake could sleep standing up, so I guess he wasn't too put out.

Uncle Jake's head popped out of the kitchen at the first creak of the bedroom door.

"You're quite a sleeper," he said. "The day's half gone."

I was still sleepy-faced, standing in the middle of his third-floor apartment, scratching my butt. I yawned.

"Go take a pish," he ordered in his Yiddish accent. "Your breakfast is getting cold."

I smiled and quickly shuffled into the bathroom. Uncle Jake's bathroom was a little messier than the one I was used to. Water swirled continuously in the toilet and the bowl was perpetually covered with condensation. The sink was spattered with toothpaste spit, and the floor . . . well, let's just say that I washed my feet a lot that summer.

LAWRENCE KELTER

I quickly covered the seat with toilet paper, a luxury my traveling parents could not take for granted, and sat down to transact my morning business.

The floor tiles were those little, white, eight-sided jobs set into black grout. They were cool and felt great beneath my feet as I tried to squeeze each of my toes into a separate tile. I normally sit down to pee when I'm too sleepy to see straight. Mom doesn't like it when I miss. You remember my mom, don't you? She's the woman whose life work was visiting a continent that didn't have any toilet paper. Okay, that's probably getting old. No more toilet paper remarks, I promise.

I yanked down my pajamas and let go. Peeing can be such a joy. At my age, penile stimulation only ranks from good to great. There's no such thing as a negative experience (unless, I suppose, you drop a bowling ball on it. Thank God I'm not that clumsy). I've devised three classifications of penis pleasure: whizzing, whacking, and the other thing—you know, that elusive and unattainable thing that all boys my age dream about twenty-four hours a day. I had yet to experience it, but in terms of mental preparation, I was more than ready.

But I was not ready for breakfast . . . well, not this breakfast anyway, not an Uncle Jake breakfast. By the way, Uncle Jake was the tallest old man I had ever seen. I mean I was five-nine already, not exactly a peanut for my age. He seemed like a giant as I stared up at him from my chair at the kitchen table. He was six three or so he said; I think he was taller. He looked as tall as Dave DeBusschere, the Knick's power forward who I saw face-to-face when the two of us got off the flight from Los Angeles together. I'm a big fan of his and wear the same sneakers too: Adidas Super Star, which may not seem like much to you, but there weren't too many kids wearing thirty-dollar leather sneakers in 1969, certainly not in Brooklyn. Anyway, I got DeBusschere's autograph on a cocktail napkin—a cocktail napkin, which I had absentmindedly left on the kitchen table last night and was now smeared with butter. By the way, DeBusschere was six foot six.

"I shut your air conditioner when I got up this morning," he said. "Your room was freezing cold. I didn't want you to get sick and have your father complain I'm not taking good care of you."

Somehow the idea of Uncle Jake tiptoeing into the bedroom while I was sleeping gave me the creeps. Granted, it was his bedroom; still and all, a man of my sensitive years needs his privacy. "I like it cold. We have central air-conditioning at home."

"Well, I'm not a big-shot Hollywood producer like your father. The electricity costs a fortune. Besides, you'll get sick."

"Isn't that an old wives' tale?"

"Never mind an old wives' tale; you'll catch pneumonia."

"Is it okay if I open the window?"

"If you're strong enough. They were painted shut and stick a little. I need a paint job, but the landlord's a miser."

"Why don't you call a lawyer?"

"This isn't Beverly Hills. It's Brooklyn," Uncle Jake grumbled. "What kind of *schlemiel* calls a lawyer to get a paint job? He'll get the message if I'm late paying the rent," he explained.

The white-gloss kitchen walls had yellowed, cracked, and peeled. Spider webs, thick enough to support a circus high-wire act, covered the ceiling.

Uncle Jake hovered over me with an old, dented pot. I noticed that his forearms were as thick as tree limbs as he scooped out a huge ladle full of oatmeal and plopped it into my dish. He had probably cooked it at 6:00 a.m., or whenever it was that people his age woke up. The consistency was somewhere between vulcanized rubber and partially set concrete.

"What's the matter?" he asked.

"I didn't say anything."

"You wrinkled your nose," he complained. "What's wrong, you don't like oatmeal?"

"It's kind of a hot day for oatmeal."

"It's good for you. I fed it to your father for years."

"My father hates oatmeal."

Uncle Jake seemed surprised by the news. He didn't know that my dad used to flush it down the toilet the moment Uncle Jake left for work. "How could that be?" he asked. I just kept quiet and let him figure it out on his own. "Oh," he said after a moment. "He never complained."

At this point, I suppose I should fill in the blanks. Uncle Jake raised my dad after Grandpa Ted, my dad's dad, died in the Battle of the Bulge. By the way, my name is Josh Stern. My dad's Robert Stern, my mom's Wendy Stern, and Uncle Jake . . . yes, you guessed it: he's the sternest of us all. My dad, the big-shot Hollywood producer, thinks that's funny.

"I would have gone out for fresh bagels, but I didn't want to leave you asleep in a strange place," he said. "I know you can't get good bagels in California."

"Sure we can," I said defensively.

"*Feh.* They've got garbage out there. You need Brooklyn water. California steals everything from Brooklyn, but it's not as good. The Dodgers, the Giants, they took them all, the *gonifs,* and now they all stink . . . just like the bagels." Uncle Jake walked to the stove, turned off the flame, and set the pot of rubber on the cooling burner. "I'll get fresh tomorrow on the way home from *shul.*" Uncle Jake ran the water in the kitchen sink and hocked up a huge chunk of phlegm.

"*Shul?*" I asked.

"Of course, *shul,*" he said. "You packed a suit, I hope."

"Uh-no."

"*Oy,*" he sighed. "A clean pair of trousers and a shirt?"

"Yes."

"That'll do. The temple's not air-conditioned anyway."

I tasted the oatmeal. Its texture was not unlike wet sand. "You go every week?"

"God willing," Uncle Jake said, standing over me. "How's the oatmeal?"

"It's okay."

He smiled. "You'll get used to it, right?" I nodded. I mean what could I say? He examined my hair. "You're a good looking boy, but you could use a trim, no?"

"I don't know," I said, hoping he could read between the lines. I liked my hair long; long hair was kind of "in" back home. How did teenagers wear their hair in Brooklyn, with ducktails and Brylcream like in those beach-party movies?

"You'll come with me to Al the barber. I go every Friday."

I made a mental note to be less subtle. Apparently it was best to take the direct approach with Uncle Jake. I was wondering why Uncle Jake got a haircut every week. Three strands of white hair covered his heavily tanned skull. The tufts growing out of his ears were thicker than the hair over his temples. "You don't need a haircut." I thought he might take the hint.

"I go for a shave." Uncle Jake plopped down in the chair next to me. "There's nothing like it," he said. "The feeling of the hot towel on your face and the crisp edge of steel." He ran his fingers over his beard, closed his eyes, and smiled. "It's wonderful." He reached forward and examined my chin. "You're not ready yet." He turned my head from side to side. "Soon," he opined. "I'll ask Al to give you a hot towel anyway, after he cuts your hair." The hot towel sounded pretty good. I made a snap judgment and decided that Uncle Jake was way past his penis pleasure days.

Maybe I was still being too subtle. "I'm not sure I want my hair cut, Uncle Jake."

"Don't be silly," he said as he stood. "You can't go to *shul* looking like that Ringo *putz*." Really, did he just criticize one of the Beatles? "Just a trim," he said as he picked up the newspaper and tucked it under his arm. "You don't need the toilet right now, do you?"

I shook my head.

"Good." He clutched his gut. "The oatmeal works fast." He took a few steps, stopped, and then turned back to me. "Don't go barefoot in the bathroom. I put down roach powder to kill the water bugs." He turned away and didn't see me cringe as I scraped the soles of my feet on the kitchen linoleum.

What I would soon find out is that every window in his apartment was painted shut and that they're much tougher to open when you're gasping for air.

CHAPTER TWO

"**H**ello, Jake." Al the barber greeted Uncle Jake enthusiastically, grinning from ear to ear. Al was a tiny black man with nappy gray hair. He was buzzing a huge guy with red hair, whom I would learn was an Irishman named Kelley.

"You're in a good mood," Uncle Jake said. "What's happening, the pomade's moving this week?"

"Ha, ha," Al cackled as he pushed Kelley's head forward to buzz the back of his thick, red neck.

Kelley looked up at us from the corner of his eye while his head was facing the floor. "Hello, Stern," he said.

"Kelley," Uncle Jake replied. "I thought I spotted your truck outside." Kelley's soda truck was visible through the barbershop window. Later on, Uncle Jake told me that he took the truck home with him at night. I could tell straight off that he wasn't one of Uncle Jake's favorites.

"I've got a special on seltzer this week, Stern," Kelley said.

"I've still got plenty," Uncle Jake replied.

"Don't keep it too long, it goes flat," Kelley told him.

Uncle Jake covered his mouth with his fist and pretended to cough. "Like your head," he mumbled.

Uncle Jake put his hand on my shoulder and ushered me forward. "This is my nephew Josh, Bob's son. He's staying with me for the summer," he boasted.

Kelley waved to me without saying a word.

"Bob's son?" Al was astonished. "Oh dear Lord, where has the time gone?" Al turned off the trimmer and walked over to shake my hand. "Pleased to meet you, Josh. I used to cut your dad's hair before he moved to California and became a big Hollywood success. He still got that thick head of black hair?"

"He's a little gray now."

"Little Bobby Stern's got gray hair? My, my." Al shook his head in disbelief. "I bet he gets a good haircut being in the movie business and all."

"He says no one cuts his hair the way you did," I said.

"He does?" Al seemed oh-so-pleased with the compliment.

"Yup," I replied. "He says that the studio hairdressers don't know what to do with his thick hair."

"My, my." You could see that I had made him really happy. "Have a seat, gentlemen. It'll just be a minute."

Uncle Jake and I took our seats, and Al went back to buzzing Kelley's neck.

Al's shop had mint-green walls and smelled like hair stuff. His counter was lined with bottles of Wild Root and Clubman. Al sang while he finished up with Kelley. It was a song I had heard, but didn't know who sang it—"Under the Boardwalk" or something.

Uncle Jake nudged me as Kelley got up from the chair. "He's a lush," he whispered. "Look at his red nose."

Kelley was a huge man, with a potbelly that hung over the belt of his green uniform pants. He saluted Uncle Jake as he walked out. "Stern," he said.

"Kelley," Uncle Jake replied. "Did you see his beer belly?" he asked me after Kelley had left.

"Yes."

"His wife left him," Uncle Jake said. "He got so drunk, he hit her in the mouth and knocked out her teeth. Dr. Botstein had to make her a partial. He's such a *zhlub*." He looked out at the street to make sure Kelley was gone and then turned to Al, "Why you don't slip and cut his throat the next time you give him a shave?"

"Ah, Jake," Al said, "You shouldn't be talking trouble. It'll only come back to haunt you."

"Feh," Uncle Jake said, waving his hand dismissively. "Believe me, he wouldn't be missed."

Al shook Kelley's hair off the barber's cape. "Okay, who's first?" he asked.

"Josh will go first," Uncle Jake said. "Give him a hot towel when you're finished."

"Sure thing," Al said.

I got up and reluctantly walked to the chair. Al winked at me as I sat down. "Good to see a young man that wants to look neat. Getting so the young folks don't want to cut their hair hardly at all. Either that or they go to those sissy women's salons." Al played with my hair, examining the texture. "You got nicer hair than your pop, young man. What'll it be?"

"Just a little off the top, please."

"Little off the top, coming up." Al smiled as he draped the cape over me. "This'll be the best haircut you ever got."

God, I hope so.

"How do you like Brooklyn so far?"

"There's a lot more concrete than I expected."

"I suppose you got lots of green grass out by you?"

"Lots," I agreed, nodding.

"How do you like it otherwise?"

"I only got here last night. Uncle Jake took me home from the airport and I went to sleep." Al examined the scissors on the counter. I cringed as he reached for a big one, but then he reconsidered and picked up the smallest one. *Yes.*

"All the way from California, you must be good and tired."

"He slept twelve hours," Uncle Jake volunteered. "I was ready to call the funeral parlor."

Al cackled. "Your uncle's a real kidder. Ha, ha . . . California, my, my, I ain't never been out west. I'd like to get out there one day though."

"Who in their right mind would want to? I went out there to visit. Such a bunch of *gonifs*." Uncle Jake blurted. "The Mets are going to murder the Dodgers this year . . . the Giants too."

"The Dodgers ain't the same since Koufax retired," Al said.

"*Feh*, another traitor who left Brooklyn. I got no use for him . . . Too bad though, a nice Jewish boy like that. He refused to pitch on Yom Kippur you know."

"They say his shoulder went bad . . . or was it his elbow?"

"His elbow," Uncle Jake replied. "What do you expect? The smog will do that to you. I don't see how the people in Los

Angeles can live. You can't breathe. The body gets weak and breaks down."

"What about it, young man?" Al asked. "You have any trouble breathing?" He laughed as he pointed at Uncle Jake. "Your uncle don't like California too much, ever since the Dodgers moved out of Ebbets Field . . . He's sure got some strong opinions, don't he?"

I nodded. "I don't have any problem breathing."

"See that, Jake, your nephew don't have no problems with the air . . . unless, of course, his uncle breaks wind. Ha, ha." Uncle Jake's flatulence was the stuff of legends.

"Funny. Are you a comedian or a barber?" Uncle Jake asked. "Right now I can't tell which. Make sure you clean him up good; he's going to *shul* with me tomorrow. Give him his money's worth."

"The boy just wants a trim, Jake," Al said. "I ain't gonna scalp him." Oh, I liked Al. I liked him a lot. "Say, that Seaver's a heck of a pitcher, ain't he, Jake?"

"He's murder. His curveball looks like it's rolling off the end of a table."

"He's Jewish too, ain't he, Jake?"

"Nah. Everyone thinks he's Jewish because his name is Seaver, but he's a gentile, like all the other athletes today."

I watched Al's progress in the mirror. Happily, the snippets of hair he was cutting were small. Before I knew it, he was combing my hair into place.

"How's that?" Al asked.

"Take off some more," Uncle Jake barked.

"Won't do it, Jake. If I take off too much, the boy won't want to come back."

I turned my head from side to side as I looked in the mirror. Aside from the dorky way that Al had combed it, it wasn't too bad, and I knew I could easily fix it once I got home. I nodded happily.

"Satisfied?" he asked. I nodded again. "Scoot on over to the next chair so that I can start on your uncle, and I'll wrap you up in a nice hot towel."

Al took a hot towel out of the boiler, sprinkled it with Old Spice, and wrapped it around my face. At first I thought it would sear my skin right off, but I got used to it after a minute and started to enjoy the experience. It was warm, private, and smelled great. It felt so good, I felt like falling asleep. Perhaps I did nod off for a while, but I could still hear Uncle Jake and Al jabbering away in the background.

"How you feeling, Jake? You're getting darker and darker every time I see you."

"What's a matter, afraid I'm giving you a run for your money?"

"You're dark, Jake, but you ain't that dark. Ha, ha. You know you ain't supposed to stay out in the sun *that much*; some folks say it ain't healthy for you."

"Nothing's good for you . . . the most delicious foods are the worst things for you. In the entire world, there's nothing better than a good pastrami sandwich, but too much of it . . . and chicken *schmaltz*?" he stopped, clasped his hands to his cheeks and shook his head from side to side. "Instant heart attack. Besides, I love the sun."

"Don't seem natural, a white man as dark as you."

"My father was dark."

"You must be one of them black Jews."

"A Sephardic?" Uncle Jake grumbled. "I'm not a goddamn Sephardic. My father was born in Russia."

"Take it easy, Jake. Don't make sense to get worked up while a black man has a razor pressed against your throat."

Uncle Jake chuckled. "Some black man, I'm almost blacker than you are. Ah, what a shame I ruined my vision in the war. Can you imagine the kind of ballplayer I would have been? I would have been Hank Greenberg before Hank Greenberg was Hank Greenberg. I would have been the Jewish Jackie Robinson."

"Yeah, Hank Greenberg was a good ballplayer all right. He wasn't no Willie Mays though."

"What are you talking about? Hank

Greenberg was the best power hitter that ever lived. It sounded like a mortar blast when he hit the ball. He would have broken Ruth's record in 1938 if all of baseball wasn't against him."

"What's that about, Jake?"

"Come on, you don't know? They wouldn't pitch to him, the bastards. They didn't want a Jew breaking Babe Ruth's homerun record."

"That a fact?"

"Absolutely."

"Willie Mays was still better."

"Go on, you're dreaming."

I guess it was their highly emotional conversation that brought me around. In any case, the towel was now cool, which felt good too. It wasn't up there with penis pleasure, but a hot towel now and again was definitely something I could get used to.

I had never heard of Hank Greenberg. For that matter, I had never heard of any Jewish ballplayer other than Sandy Koufax. My folks were not very religious. All the same, it made me proud to know that a Jewish athlete had been so good. Before I knew it, Al was pulling the towel off my face.

"How'd you like your first hot towel?" Al asked.

"I liked it."

"Wait until you raise a beard, that's when you'll first appreciate how good it is,"

Uncle Jake said. "That's when you'll really feel like a man."

We were out of Al's barbershop and halfway down the block before we spoke again.

"Uncle Jake, was Hank Greenberg really a better baseball player than Willie Mays?" I waited eagerly for his confirmation. I had never been so excited about being Jewish.

"You don't know much about baseball, do you?"

"I like watching it."

"But you don't play?"

"I'm not much of a hitter."

"So your father can't work with you on this? It's in our blood after all."

"You were good, weren't you, Uncle Jake? My dad said you used to hit the ball a mile."

"Me?" I could see that he was recalling a memory. After a moment, he put his arm around me. "I love the game."

"Why didn't you become a professional?"

"Professional? Are you crazy? You know how many Jews there were in baseball when I was a young man?" I shook my head. "Zero, none, *goonisht*. The blacks tell you about Jackie Robinson all the time, but it was even worse for the Jews. Besides, I came back from the war with a detached retina. After that, I played like a *schlemiel*."

"But what about Hank Greenberg?"

Uncle Jake squinted at me. "You mean, was he better than Willie Mays?"

"I heard you tell Al that he was."

"What are you kidding me? Willie Mays was the greatest baseball player that ever lived: eleven Golden Glove Awards, two MVPs, and six hundred-sixty home runs."

"But you said—"

"Yeah, yeah, yeah. I know what I said." He patted me on the back. "I'm a Jew, it comes with the territory."

CHAPTER THREE

Uncle Jake had a drawer full of *yarmulkes* and an extra *tallit*, which I brought with me on my first visit to his *shul*.

"Go sit over there with the young people," he said, "and try not to look out of place."

The back rows of the *shul* were filled with kids my age. I kissed the corners of the *tallit* like everyone else did before putting it on my shoulders and took a seat in the corner of the very last row, trying my best not to stand out.

I looked over at Uncle Jake, who was seated with the older men. He must have felt my eyes on him because he turned to me, raised a copy of the prayer book for me to see, and pointed to it. There were several in the bench holder in front of me. I grabbed the closest one and opened it up. Uncle Jake nodded with approval before turning away.

I had only been to temple a few times in my life and never to one like this, where all the prayers were recited in Hebrew. You see, my mom's only half Jewish and my dad . . . well, I think he got his fill of Judaism living with Uncle Jake. Anyway, religion wasn't a big thing in our home. After all, there was all this talk about eating frog's legs and snails once they got to Paris. I didn't know much about Jewish dietary laws, but I was pretty sure that stuff wasn't exactly kosher.

Attendance was light. There was half a bench-length between the next worshipper and me, which was good because after an hour or so the jetlag really hit me, and I . . . well, to be honest, I fell asleep. I mean, I tried following the few English sentences I found on each page of the prayer book, but for Pete's sake, the Jews don't even read from left to right.

I felt someone nudging me. "Five more minutes, Mom, please," I said. I heard giggling, but when I opened my eyes, I wasn't home in bed, and it wasn't my mom's familiar smile that greeted me.

"Your uncle sent me over to help you out." The most beautiful, dark-haired girl was sitting next to me. "You were snoring," she whispered. She had these incredible, electric-green eyes that flashed every time she smiled.

"Oh my God, was I?"

She nodded. "Are all California boys as disrespectful as you are?" I was so embarrassed about having fallen asleep that I didn't know how to respond. "I said are all you California boys as disrespectful as you are?" she repeated.

"I'm not disrespectful, I'm, I'm—"

"Come on, surfer boy, spit it out." The volume of her voice was low, but insistent.

She slipped off her blazer. Much to my delight, she had a very full chest—the kind that boys my age can't get enough of. "My name's Rachel," she said, extending her hand, "but everyone calls me Rocky."

What an unusual name for a girl, I thought. I immediately realized that an entirely new category needed to be added to my list of penis pleasures: ogling. Just looking at Rocky made me feel tingly all over, which was not bad for my first real religious experience. "Rocky?"

"That's what I said, surfer boy. Rocky. It's short for Rochelle *(Ra-hale)*, which is my Hebrew name."

"I'm not a surfer boy," I said.

"Well, why not? Isn't that what they do in California?" Before I could reply, she pointed to the rabbi. "Stand up," she whispered. "They're going to walk by with the Torah. When they pass, touch it with your prayer book and then kiss the book."

Sure enough, the rabbi, cantor, and the other men from around the bema began circulating through the temple, carrying the Torah. The worshippers all began making their way to the ends of their aisles so that they could reach out and touch the Torah as it came by.

I was reaching for it when I felt Rocky's boobs pressing against me. I'm sure it was inadvertent and that she was only leaning against me so that she could touch the Torah. Be that as it may, I felt my blood pressure skyrocket and my face grow flush. When Rocky said touch it, I didn't think she meant with my penis, but that was within the realm of possibility. Thank God the Jewish people don't believe in hell and eternal damnation.

For the next twenty minutes, I stood when Rocky stood, turning pages when she did, and never once took my eyes from her incredible breasts.

I did break my gaze once when I saw that Uncle Jake was looking at me again, nodding with approval. I smiled back. *Shul* was not so bad after all. I glanced at Rocky's chest again. I thought I was being inconspicuous, but this time I got caught.

"Hey, are all you California kids as rude as you are?" she asked.

I shook my head. "What do you mean?"

"For God's sake, surfer boy, you haven't stopped staring at my chest since the moment you opened your eyes. Avert your eyes please. I'm the rabbi's daughter, you know."

The rabbi's daughter? Oh God, this is bad. "I haven't been staring." I tried to look innocent, but her chest was constantly heaving, out and back. My pulse rose and fell with every breath she took. "Honest," I said, but the situation was hopeless. "Are you really the rabbi's daughter?"

She glared at me. "That's what I said."

My prayer book was lying in my lap. Rocky picked it up, turned to the correct page, and pointed to the place the service was up to.

"Thanks," I said, but despite my every effort, my eyes kept wandering back to her chest. After a moment, I forced myself to make eye contact. "I don't know Hebrew."

Rocky's eyes widened with surprise. "No?" I shook my head. "You're not preparing for your bar mitzvah?" I shook my head again. Was this the only thing these people ever thought about? "That's a *shande*," she said, whatever that meant. "You'll never become a man."

"What are you talking about?"

"Your testicles will never descend, you stupid surfer boy. What do you think every boy prays for at his bar mitzvah?" she whispered. I shrugged. "He prays that his testicles will descend and he'll become a man."

"That's baloney."

"If you don't become a bar mitzvah, you'll never become a man, and you'll never be able to father a child."

"You're full of it."

"Really, you couldn't even admit you were staring at my boobs."

Did she say boobs?

Rocky turned forward. The congregation rose and so did we, both of us trying to appear as if we were following the proceedings.

"Watch me and pretend you know what you're doing," she said indignantly.

I mimicked her every movement. All the time, I was thinking of what to say, a way to regain some shred of dignity, but all I came up with was, "I really wasn't staring."

To which she replied, "Why not, aren't you a man?" I thought I saw a hint of a smile as she said that. As naïve as I was, I knew enough to know she was toying with me. I sighed. "Don't worry," she continued. "I'll groom you."

I gave her what must have been the dumbest look in the history of the world. "For what?"

"You silly surfer boy, I'm going to groom you to become a man."

I had no idea what Rocky was talking

about, but what with being so close to her and all the talk about achieving sexual maturity, I got so excited I almost did something unmentionable in my boxers.

The rest of the services seemed to go by quickly. There were much fewer prayers and far more songs, which I lip-synched in the best tradition of Japanese filmmaking. You know what I mean, my lips moved a split-second behind the words of the songs, like in those poorly dubbed Godzilla movies: *Godzilla is attacking Tokyo, prepare the high-tension wires,* but the actor's mouth doesn't stop moving until seconds after the last word is uttered.

The service finally ended, three hours after it had begun. "Well, that's it," Rocky said. "Will you stay for the *Kiddush*?" she asked. "We don't have any avocados."

"I don't like avocado."

"Oh," she said in a snide manner. "I thought everyone from California likes them."

"Well, I don't."

"So are you staying or going?"

"I don't know."

"Well, what do you want to do? You said you were a man so you should be able to make up your own mind. Your uncle usually stays."

"Then I guess I will too."

"Good," she said. Rocky put on her blazer and extended her hand. With her chest concealed, I finally found the opportunity to take another long look at her face. She was very cute. "I'll see you inside then," she said coolly. She filed out toward the opposite end of the aisle. My heart sank. The room seemed to grow darker.

I made my way towards the exit.

"So? How was it?" Suddenly, Uncle Jake was standing in front of me. I hadn't even noticed him approaching.

"It was okay. What's a *Kiddush*?"

"*Chiam Yankel*, this is your first time to a synagogue? You're almost a bar mitzvah."

I was too embarrassed to ask him what *chiam yankel* meant, and certainly too embarrassed to tell him that there was no bar mitzvah in my future. "We don't go to temple much."

Uncle Jake's mouth dropped. "You're not preparing for your bar mitzvah?" A group of men were filing out. I shook my head in the most inconspicuous manner possible. Uncle Jake rolled his eyes. A man with an unpleasant-looking face stopped to introduce himself. "Hello, Perelman," Uncle Jake said.

"So who's this?" Perelman said, displaying excessive curiosity.

"This is my nephew Josh," Uncle Jake replied. "He's staying with me for the summer. His parents are in Europe."

"Europe?" he said, rocking his head from side to side. "Joshua the savior?" he asked. I shrugged. I guess I looked pretty stupid not knowing what he was talking about. Perelman turned to Uncle Jake, looking at him as if he was about to impose sentencing.

"You're so mixed up?" Uncle Jake said to me, playfully showing me the back of his hand. "From the bible—" He turned back to Perelman. "Jetlag. He flew in late last night."

"Ah," Perelman said, seeming satisfied with the excuse. He turned back to me. "You'll have beautiful discussions with the rabbi about your namesake."

"I'm looking forward to it," I said. Perelman nodded from the shoulders. He looked like an undertaker.

"Such a big boy," Perelman continued. "A *groyse shtarker.*"

"You should see him play baseball," Uncle Jake bragged. "He hits the ball like Mickey Mantle."

Perelman didn't see me looking at Uncle Jake like he was crazy.

"See you both inside," Perelman said as he slinked off.

"Why'd you say that?" I asked.

Uncle Jake shrugged. "What did you want me to tell him, that you play like a *shlemiel*?"

Uncle Jake took me by the arm and led me into the lobby where he found a quiet place to talk. "Why didn't you tell me you know *bupkis* about your religion? Perelman's the biggest *yente* in the temple; in five minutes, the whole congregation will know that you're not studying for your bar mitzvah."

I pushed his hand off my arm. "I'm sorry," I said unhappily. "No one told me I'd have to go to temple with you every week. My parents don't make me do it, so why should I have to go with you? This is my vacation."

"Come on, Joshua. It's an embarrassment for me. I've been worshipping here for decades. You fell asleep during services."

"I was exhausted."

"Please," he said with exasperation.

My lack of faith had never bothered me, but now, for the first time ever, I felt guilty about not fulfilling my obligation as a Jew. "Why should it bother you? It doesn't bother my parents."

"This I can't believe. You're willing to grow up without a faith?"

"Yes! Now leave me alone." My words were loud enough to turn heads. I wasn't making a great first impression on the congregation.

"Shush," Uncle Jake said. "I'm sorry. I didn't realize. I thought you'd be preparing for your bar mitzvah like any other Jewish boy your age."

"Well, I'm not."

"I said I'm sorry. Calm down. Come into the *Kiddush* room and have something to eat. We can talk about this later."

"I'd rather go home."

"And miss the *Kiddush*?" This seemed to shock Uncle Jake. "Come take a look. There's delicious food inside."

"You go," I said unhappily. "Enjoy yourself."

"Ay. I see you've got a temper. All right, here." Uncle Jake reached into his pocket and handed me his house keys. "You won't get lost?"

I was still glaring at him. "I think I can handle it." I took the house keys and walked off.

"See you later," he said, calling after me. "There's tuna fish in the cupboard. Make yourself some lunch. Don't lose the keys." His words seared my ears as I pushed open the temple heavy doors and escaped to the outside world.

As I walked past the temple, I passed the *Kiddush* room and saw Rocky through the window. She was talking to another boy, smiling, and curling her hair around her finger. I wanted to be that other guy so badly that I didn't see where I was and walked into a johnny pump, bumping my shin. I rubbed it for a moment. When I looked up, Rocky was looking out the window at me, fighting to hold back her laughter.

I cursed myself for my pigheadedness and hurried off. I wanted plenty of time alone before Uncle Jake got home. All I could think about was Rocky and about lying back on Uncle Jake's bed and whacking off.

CHAPTER FOUR

By the time Uncle Jake got home, Rocky had surrendered to me not once, but twice. I had taken her in my bed at home and once in the coatroom at the *shul*—in my head, anyway.

Sacrilege. I had defiled my uncle's sanctuary and God's as well. I felt like my crimes were so severe that perhaps in my case, even the Jews would make an exception and agree to an eternal sentencing in hell.

My folks had given me strict instructions not to bother Uncle Jake with petty chores like my laundry. To that end, I had brought along my own laundry sack, within which a telltale pair of soiled Ban-Lon socks had now been stashed.

Uncle Jake was dripping wet as he walked into the bedroom. One burning question weighed heavily on my mind. "Uncle Jake, what does *shande* mean?"

Uncle Jake's suit jacket was draped over his shoulder. He threw it on the bed and sat down sidesaddle. He seemed very concerned. "Where'd you hear this word?"

"Someone at the temple said it."

"Who? Tell me who? Was it Perelman? He's such a sourpuss."

"It wasn't Perelman. It was Rocky."

"Sweet little Rocky? She said a thing like this? What were you talking about?"

I wanted to drop the subject. I wanted to turn on the ball game and let my guilt fade away, but I didn't. "She asked me if I was preparing for my bar mitzvah and—"

"*Oy yoy yoy*, this business again? Look, I'm sorry. I had no business questioning you in the temple like that. Sure, I'd like to discuss this more, but not like that . . . I was out of line."

"You're not going to tell me what it means?"

"*Shande? Shande* means shame. It's nothing, really. Like I would say it's a *shande* the Dodgers left Brooklyn. That's all. Forget about it." Uncle Jake waved his hand dismissively. *"Feh."* I guess I looked pretty unhappy. "Such a sad face; it's nothing, really."

"I think Rocky was disappointed with me."

Uncle Jake thought for a minute. "What would you expect? In her world this is practically unheard of. She *is* the rabbi's daughter."

Don't ask me why, but I was very excited about having had my way with such a pious girl, even though I was going to burn in hell for it. My seed-soiled socks were probably bursting into flames at that very moment.

"She was looking for you at the *Kiddush*. I told her you had to make an important phone call to Los Angeles," Uncle Jake said in a tone that suggested importance.

"You did?"

"Sure. She got wild when I mentioned it. She thinks you're a movie star."

"She does?"

"Sure. I told her you're a regular on *American Bandstand*. That's a television show, isn't it?"

I nodded. Uncle Jake's bravado was making me feel so good. God, I was such a loser. It's a good thing I packed plenty of extra socks.

"So tell me, did you eat something?"

"I'm not really hungry," I said as I rubbed my head.

Uncle Jake picked up a brown paper bag. "The rabbi's wife packed a bagel with a *shmear* of cream cheese. Try it. It's fresh."

"Maybe later."

"Later? Later it will be rock hard." *You mean like the oatmeal?* "Eat it now while it's fresh." I shook my head. He sniffed the air. "What smells in here?"

"That's my cologne," I said sheepishly. I had been found out. How could I tell him his room smelled like a sulfur mine?

"Funny, I didn't notice it before."

I shrugged.

Uncle Jake smiled introspectively. "I'll tell you a funny joke. It's a little bit racy, but we're men here, no?" I was anxious to hear his joke. I quickly nodded. "Okay. Two *alter kakers* are sitting on a bench down in Florida. Max turns to his friend Irving and says, 'Irving, tell me, you can still get an erection?'"

I found this really thrilling; no adult had ever used a word like erection in my presence. Uncle Jake smiled. I think he saw the excitement in my expression.

"So Irving says, 'Sure. I still get hard as a rock.' 'Really?' Max says. 'What's your secret?' 'Rye bread,' Irving says." Uncle Jake turned to me. "How am I doing so far?"

"Good," I said eagerly. Sharing the joke with me made me feel like an adult.

"Well, the next day, Max goes to the supermarket. He fills his shopping cart to the top with rye bread. The checkout girl takes one look and says, 'My God. What are you going to do with all that? Don't you know that after a few days it gets hard?' And Max shouts, 'Oh, you know the secret too.'"

I roared.

"You liked it?" I nodded happily. "Good. I tell you what; why don't we go down to the playground. I'll show you how to tear the cover off a baseball."

"I thought you couldn't see well enough anymore?"

"I said I couldn't play professional, but I'm good enough to teach a *pisher* like you."

"*Pisher*?"

"*Pisher*. Wet behind the ears," he said most matter-of-fact, "You'll get used to my Yiddish in no time." Uncle Jake gave me a loving pat on the leg. "Tonight I'll take you to Kalinsky's for brisket," he said with a broad smile. "After all, you're on vacation, no?"

I had never eaten brisket, but I was smiling all the same. I guess it was his sheer exuberance that meant so much. "Okay."

Uncle Jake stood up. "Good, I'll go change my clothes. You've got something lightweight to wear? This isn't like Los Angeles where the sun can't burn through the smog. Here the sun is murder."

Why, I wondered, did he hate LA so intensely? "I brought shorts."

"Good. Give me ten minutes to change. You don't need the toilet, do you?" I shook my head. Uncle Jake made a sour face. "Too much herring."

I made a beeline for the window.

CHAPTER FIVE

The Mets were sending three men to the All-Star game that year: Seaver and Koosman, their two ace pitchers, and Cleon Jones, their best hitter. From the way things were going in the playground, it didn't look like I was going to be an All-Star any time soon.

"Swing . . . Swing . . . Swing." Uncle Jake continued to lob the ball to me time after time, and time after time, I missed. "Just watch the ball," he would say and then at the right moment, "Swing." Nothing helped. "Swing. *Oy yoy yoy.*" Then finally, "Let me show you."

Uncle Jake walked in from the mound. "Learn to relax," he said. "Don't be so nervous. It's only you and me out here."

Uncle Jake took the bat out of my hand. "The most important thing is to be relaxed. You'll never hit the ball if you're so nervous. Hold the bat loosely, watch the pitch, and swing level. That's all it takes. How's your fielding?"

"Okay, I guess."

"Take my glove, and I'll hit you a few fly balls."

He made it look so easy. I couldn't understand what was wrong with me. He did say it was in my blood, didn't he? Maybe I needed a transfusion. He was seventy years old, tossing the ball into the air and swatting it deep into the outfield with no effort at all.

My fielding was no better. "Try to judge the distance," he yelled. "I'll hit it right to you."

And he did, but I didn't catch a one. The sun was hot as hell and blaring right into my eyes. I've never been great, but I played like a total buffoon in front of him. In the back of my mind, I couldn't help thinking that I had done too much jerking off after *shul* and it was playing havoc with my coordination.

I saw the look of disappointment on his face, but he never said a disparaging word about the way I played. I guess after a while he couldn't take it anymore. "Let's take a break," he said, calling to me in the outfield. "It's too hot."

I walked in. We collected the gear and began walking home. Uncle Jake looked down at my sneakers. "What kind of sneakers are these? No wonder you can't get to the ball. You haven't got a pair of Keds like all the other boys?"

"These are professional basketball shoes. Dave DeBusschere wears these," I said proudly.

"Who?"

"Dave DeBusschere," I repeated. "He's the starting forward for the New York Knicks."

"Basketball? This is not a sport, grown men running around in short pants." He shrugged. "I saw the Harlem Globetrotters one time. Very entertaining, but not a sport," he said dismissively. "I'll buy you a pair of Keds. It will be my present to you. These shoes you can't wear for baseball." He turned away. I could see there was no convincing him otherwise.

We stopped at Friedman's, the neighborhood grocer, for sodas, and sat down on cantaloupe crates to drink them.

Uncle Jake was looking at me while I guzzled. He was smiling. "You can't excel at athletics without proper rest and nutrition," he said. "We'll try again in a few days when you're feeling more like yourself."

"I really don't play much better than this."

He waved his hand dismissively. *"Feh.* I'm sure you can do better. The trouble is no one ever took the time to show you how. By the time you go back to California, you'll be hitting the ball like Joe DiMaggio."

"That would be nice."

"It's a given," he said most matter of fact. "A big boy like you—" Uncle Jake patted me on the leg. "You need to have a little *chutzpah.* You know what this means? You need to have a little guts and self-confidence. You have to believe in yourself. Faith is what I'm talking about. You take the best ballplayer—I don't care how much God-given talent he has, you take away his self-confidence and he'll fall on his face. I've seen it a hundred times."

I looked up at Uncle Jake hopefully. "You really think so?"

He gave me a reassuring smile. "Absolutely." I could see that he was recalling from his memory. "Your grandpa Ted, my baby brother, he was the same way: couldn't hit the ball for nothing. I taught him. *He* could have been professional. He was as fast as a bandit, your grandpa Ted. Every single, he stretched into a triple. So fast . . . *Oy,*" he sighed. "Not fast enough." I saw Uncle Jake mist over. He shook his head sadly. "Not fast enough. No *mazel.*"

"Are you all right?" I asked.

He nodded, looking sad. He brightened almost immediately. "When I get through with you, you'll be fantastic. A few days rest and some good food is what you need. We'll make a good start tonight at Kalinsky's. Everyone goes there on Saturday night. It's a tradition."

"Everyone?" I was fishing in order to find out if Rocky would be there too.

"Sure, the *ganse mishpacha*, the whole clan: sourpuss Perelman will be there, the rabbi and his family. You'll have a nice time. We'll eat like kings."

His enthusiasm made me smile. I saw him look at my leg.

"How'd you get that huge walnut on your leg? This just happened?" he asked.

"It's nothing," I said.

"You need some ice on that." Uncle Jake stood immediately and marched into the store. "Friedman, you *gonif*," he called. "You've got a little ice for my nephew Josh?"

It was nice of Uncle Jake to go for the ice, but the truth was that I was having an out-of-body experience and the discomfort from the bruise on my leg was unimportant. The only thing of importance was that I would soon be seeing Rocky again. I thought about the long hours I would have to wait until dinner. My stomach grumbled.

CHAPTER SIX

Uncle Jake's head hovered inches above his huge dinner plate, his neck craned downward like a vulture's as he shoveled *kasha varnishkas* into his mouth—little bowtie-shaped macaroni covered in brown muck that smelled awful. He looked up. "You're sure you don't want to try?"

"No thanks." There was a metal pot on the table filled with pickles and other horrible-looking, vinegar-soaked objects. I found a solitary half-sour gherkin in the pot, which I nibbled on while I looked around Kalinsky's Kosher Restaurant. All the walls were mirrored, which struck me as odd. I mean, who in their right mind would want to look in the mirror while they stuffed their face? The perimeter of the restaurant was lined with booths with vinyl-clad bench seats. The center of the restaurant was filled with Formica tables.

I recognized many of the faces from the morning's service. Perelman was there with his family: his brutally ugly wife Evelyn and his son Phillip, who was so excited to meet me that he yawned in my face during introductions. His butt was so big that it took up the entire booth—too many *latkes*, I guess.

"Are you sure you don't want a nice bowl of matzo ball soup?" Uncle Jake asked. Rocky was nowhere to be seen.

I shook my head. "No thanks."

"You eat like a bird," he said.

The rabbi and his family had not yet arrived. I was extremely worried that Rocky would not be making an appearance when the waitress arrived with the rest of our food. She placed Uncle Jake's brisket in front of him. "Don't touch the plate," she warned, "Very hot." Each small, ivory-colored dish contained something different. She set several in front of Uncle Jake: *kishke*, peas and carrots, fried onions, and a round knish. She set my corned beef sandwich in front of me, followed by a huge dish of French fries. "Would you like some Russian for your sandwich, Sweetheart," she asked. I shook my head. "Anything else, gentlemen?"

Uncle Jake lifted his cup. "More hot water for my tea."

"Would you like a fresh teabag?" she asked.

"No," Uncle Jake said, not wanting to be charged for another cup of tea. "Just hot water."

The waitress replied, "Be right back."

"Dig in," Uncle Jake said to me as he picked up his knife and fork. "It looks delicious."

I began picking on French fries, eating as slowly as possible. I didn't want to finish before Rocky arrived, but the food was delicious, and it was difficult not to wolf it down. After all, I hadn't eaten anything all day.

I looked up at Uncle Jake. His forehead was covered with sweat. He wiped it away with his dinner napkin and looked up at me, smiling and chewing a mouthful of brisket. A note on kosher cuisine; you can't really enjoy yourself unless you work up a good sweat while you're packing it away.

"It's delicious, no?"

"It's very good."

"You should've tried the brisket like I told you. The meat is like butter."

"I was in the mood for a sandwich."

"Next time," he said.

"I don't see the rabbi yet."

Uncle Jake cut another huge piece of meat and held it on his fork. "You're so worried about meeting the rabbi?" He made the connection an instant later. "Oh." He smiled and then ate the brisket. "Don't worry. The rabbi always comes to dinner at Kalinsky's. He'll be here."

I was down to my last French fry, the tiniest, burnt morsel, when I saw Uncle Jake's eyes light up. "They're here," he announced. He wiped his mouth and stood up, waving energetically for someone to come over.

My heart leapt. "The rabbi?" *Rocky's here?* I turned around. There she was. Our eyes met instantly, but she turned away to greet someone else. Uncle Jake was still waving. He smiled a second later. "Stand up," he said. "The rabbi's coming."

I was on my feet and facing the rabbi as he arrived. Rocky and the rabbi's wife were a few steps behind him.

"Jakela," the rabbi said, giving Uncle Jake a hearty greeting. "Is this Joshua?" Uncle Jake nodded even though the rabbi's question was rhetorical. "Ah, Joshua, who delivered our people to the Promised Land, Joshua the Savior." The rabbi took my hand and shook it heartily. He was a short man with gray hair and a ruddy complexion. He wore wire-rimmed bifocals. "It's a pleasure to meet you, young man. I can still remember when your father made his bar mitzvah. I hope he's well."

"He's very well, thank you, Rabbi."

"That's wonderful, wonderful." He finally

let go of my hand. "I hear you're going to spend the summer with your uncle. This is your first time to Brooklyn?"

"Yes, Rabbi." Conversations I had had with rabbis during the course of my life had been few; okay, there hadn't been any. For some reason, I felt that he deserved a higher level of respect than an ordinary person. I answered his every question as politely as I possibly could. The true test was making eye contact with him, all the while wanting to look at Rocky.

"You'll have a wonderful time here," he told me. "I was only in California one time, but I can tell you I liked it very much." His wife and Rocky were standing at the booth behind us, talking with another family. "Rachel, Esther, come," he said. "I want you to meet Jake's nephew Joshua."

The rabbi's wife excused herself and shook my hand. She had a very limp handshake. It was like grabbing a dead fish. "Very nice to meet you, Joshua. Such a big boy, *kenahora*." She turned her head and pretended to spit. "Poo, poo, poo." She smiled sweetly, but there was a hint of sadness in her eyes.

"I know you met my darling daughter this morning," the rabbi said as he extended his hand. Rocky took hold of it and drew closer. "Come here my *sheyne meydele*. Say hello."

Rocky stepped in front of her father and smiled, her incredible green eyes flashed more brightly than the neon sign in Kalinsky's window. "Hello, Joshua. Such a pleasure to see you again." She was a perfect lady in front of her parents. It was disappointing to think that she would not be using the word "boobs" at the dinner table this evening.

The rabbi rested his hands on Rocky's shoulders in a loving and protective manner. "What do you think of this beautiful girl, Joshua?" The rabbi gave Rocky an affectionate kiss on the cheek. "Girls like this you don't find in California."

"That's for sure," Uncle Jake interjected quickly. *What a surprise.*

Rocky blushed. Her mother stroked her cheek. Through it all, our eyes never broke contact. And then it came, the dreaded clearing of the throat. "What's going on here?" the rabbi asked playfully. "You two like one another?"

Rocky did a masterful job of exaggerating the level of her embarrassment. If only he had heard her talking during the service that morning. *"Daddy,"* she protested. "You're—"

The rabbi threw his hands in the air. "Sorry. Sorry."

The rabbi's wife said, "You're embarrassing our girl. Stop it, Josef."

The rabbi pinched Rocky's cheek. "What are fathers for? Come," he said to them. "Let's have some dinner." He looked at Uncle Jake's plate and then turned to him. "How's the brisket? Tasty?"

"Like butter," Uncle Jake replied. "I think Kalinsky's using a new butcher."

"*Oy*. I'm starving," the rabbi said. He turned to his wife. "Order some soup, Esther. I'll go wash *mine* hands." He extended his hand toward me again. "Don't be a stranger. I hope to see you in *shul*."

We shook hands and said goodbye. The rabbi walked to the back and disappeared down a long alcove that led to the bathrooms. Rocky and her mother sat down at a nearby table.

"Finish eating," Uncle Jake said as he sat down. "Everything's getting cold."

Rocky was seated with her back to me. I couldn't see those magnificent green eyes, but I could see the side of her mother's face. She was sitting next to Rocky and admiring her with fondness. She was playing with her hair and looking at her as if nothing else existed. Rocky was no ordinary girl, not to me anyway—and certainly, it seemed, not to her mother and father.

"Your corned beef will turn to rubber," Uncle Jake said.

I smiled at Uncle Jake and took a bite of

the sandwich. He was right; it was cold, but I didn't care.

CHAPTER SEVEN

Uncle Jake was determined to show me a good time. He was proud of Brooklyn and was desperate to show me how much better it was than Los Angeles. He took me to Coney Island and the aquarium in the same day. I had such a great time that he took me back to Coney Island again the next day. I played games at the arcade and won a small bowl of goldfish. We went to Nathan's and ate hotdogs and French fries that were even better than Kalinsky's. The corn on the cob was my favorite. I had never tasted anything as sweet and good before in my life. Believe it or not, I ate three entire cobs. A quick note about the passage of corn through the digestive tract: don't be alarmed when you find whole niblets in the bowl after a number two.

Uncle Jake had a good idea about what a kid likes to do. We went to the Museum of Natural History, which I liked because there was a huge exhibit on dinosaurs. We practiced baseball once more. I wasn't as bad as the first time we played, but I wasn't ready for the major league either, not by a long shot.

Despite the fact that we were busy everyday, I never once stopped thinking about Rocky. I know this is going to sound really pathetic, but I couldn't wait for the weekend—to get the Friday haircut and hot towel at Al's Barber Shop and go to *shul* with Uncle Jake on Saturday—so much so, that I picked out the shirt and slacks I was going to wear the Monday before. I pressed them, and inspected them everyday to make sure they hadn't wrinkled.

I saw Rocky at *shul* on Saturday morning, but we didn't sit together. She was sitting with some other girls, who I had no interest in whatsoever. I even went to the *Kiddush*, not to eat of course, but for the opportunity to be with her. We did talk for a few minutes, but she was busy helping serve the food. It was hard to talk with so many people around. "How are you? Nice to see you again." Anyway, you know the drill. There was no talk about body parts or coming of age. I mean, she said that she was going to groom me. When was the process going to start?

Uncle Jake stayed behind to talk with some of his friends. I was so disappointed that I didn't even whack off when I got back to his house. I turned on the baseball game as a distraction. Uncle Jake owned, what I imagined to be, the very first television ever manufactured. The screen was about six inches wide. The black-and-white picture was blurry. Horizontal lines ran up the screen from bottom to top, which made watching the game a real joy. My mood was really somber when the phone rang.

"Hello."

"Hi, Sweetheart. Hi, Josh. It's Mommy and Daddy."

My mother's voice seemed distant, as did everything else that day. The sky was cloudy as I looked out the window, the sun seemingly set further back in the sky than usual. "Hi, Mom."

"Hello, Sweetheart, I'm so glad we caught you in. How are you?" she asked.

"I'm okay. How's your trip?"

I heard my mother whispering to my dad, "He sounds terrible, Bob. I knew we shouldn't have gone." I guess I sounded pretty blue. I hadn't meant to.

I also heard my father's reply. "I'm sure he's okay. Let me talk to him."

"Not yet," she said. Then she was back on the phone. "The trip's just fine. Are you feeling all right, Josh?"

"I'm okay."

"Are you sure?" she persisted. "You don't sound like my Josh."

"I'm okay. I think I ate too much at the *Kiddush*." She must have covered the phone. I think I heard her say," Bob, he went to a *Kiddush*."

"Oh Jesus Christ," my dad swore, loud enough for me to hear him clearly. "Give me the phone."

"All right. Here," she said unhappily.

"Hi, Sport. How's it going?"

"All right."

"So the old man's dragging you to *shul* with him?" he asked.

"Yeah. I don't mind."

"Are you sure? Your uncle's a wonderful man, but you have to tell him if he wants you to do something you don't like. Believe me, I know how he can get."

"*Shul's* okay, really."

"If you're afraid to tell him, you can put him on the phone with me."

I realized my dad was never going to give up, so I figured I'd better pretend to be happy or else I'd ruin their entire vacation. "Uncle Jake took me to Coney Island twice. We went to the aquarium and the Museum of Natural History. I saw a full-size model of dinosaur poop."

I heard my dad laugh and then he whispered, "He's good. Jake took him to see all the sights. Maybe we woke him up or something."

My dad had definitely turned the corner, but I knew that he could be a tough sell, so I piled it on. "Eat any frog's legs, Dad?"

"Yes, Josh. Yes, I did."

"How were they?" There was a delay in the time it took for his response to come over the wire. I repeated myself not knowing his response was still on its way across the Atlantic. "How were they?"

"Not my favorite, but the pastry is out of this world." I shuddered, presuming the next word out of his mouth would be his butchered pronunciation of the word *croissant*. I was right. "The *croy-sense* are unbelievable." *Dear God, didn't anyone have the guts to correct him?* "Has Uncle Jake taken you to Kalinsky's yet?"

"We went on Saturday night."

"How was it?"

"We went on Saturday night." There goes that pesky cross-Atlantic delay again.

"I heard you. How was it?"

"My poop is bigger than the dinosaur's."

He was laughing again and then he whispered to my mother. "He's *fine*, eating like a horse."

"Would you let me talk to my son?"

"Josh, I'm gonna go. I'll put Mom back on. Is there anything you want to tell me?"

I was going to say something dorky like *I miss you.* I don't know where it came from, but for some reason, I asked, "Dad, how come you and Mom don't want me to have a bar mitzvah?" There was a long silence. "I said how come you and Mom don't want me to have a bar mitzvah?"

"I'm sorry, I heard you, son. I don't know. It's just that it's never been important to us, and we figured there are other things you'd rather be doing with your time."

I heard my mother say, "What are you talking about? Give me the phone."

"He's asking about a bar mitzvah," he told her. "Where's this coming from, Josh?"

The next thing I knew, my mother was back on the line. "Josh, honey, what's wrong?"

"Nothing's wrong, Mom, I just want to know why you and Dad don't want me to have a bar mitzvah? Some of my friends are having them."

"Oh gee, Josh, you've got so much to do for school. Your dad and I figured the last thing you'd want to do was worry about a silly old bar mitzvah. It's so much work and—"

"I used to think so too, but it doesn't sound silly anymore."

"What's changed, Josh?"

"Nothing. It's just something I think I'm supposed to do."

I heard my dad say, "I've got to ask him a question." He was hot when he got back on the line. "Josh, is your uncle filling your head with his nonsense about fulfilling your obligation as a Jew? Is he telling you that you won't have any faith if you don't make your bar mitzvah? Because that's exactly the same line he used on me when I objected to it. I didn't want to go for my bar mitzvah either . . . Put your uncle on the phone."

"No, Dad. It's got nothing to do with Uncle Jake at all. He's been great."

"Are you sure, Josh?"

"Yes. I'm sure. I just wanted to know. That's all. I thought it's maybe because Mom's only half-Jewish."

"That's not it, Josh. Your mom is Jewish on her mother's side, so under Jewish law, you're Jewish too. I'm sorry, son. I didn't know this was so important to you. Look, can we talk about this when we get back from Europe?"

"Sure, Dad."

"That's my boy. Here's your mom again. Enjoy your summer. We love you."

"I love you too."

I guess my question was ill timed. My mom got back on the line and gave me a full ten minutes of doting mother talk. I assured her and reassured her that I was all right and that I loved them and missed them and couldn't wait to see them again and to have a great time. They told me they'd call again soon, and I had no doubt they would. I made a mental note not to discuss religion with them on the next phone call.

For some reason, I hung up feeling reenergized. I guess it's good to get things off your chest.

Saturday night dinner at Kalinsky's lay ahead of me—and another chance to see Rocky. Someone had smacked the ball hard on the tiny TV. From the sounds of the cheering, I could tell it was headed out of the park, but with the picture so blurry, I had to use my imagination because the ball was invisible behind all of the snow.

CHAPTER EIGHT

There must have been assigned seating at Kalinsky's because Uncle Jake and I sat exactly where we had the weekend before, as did Rocky and her mother. The rabbi had not yet arrived. Rocky and Esther continually checked the restaurant's front door, anxiously awaiting his arrival.

Rocky sat facing me, her green eyes twinkling, like the two most brilliant stars I had ever seen. For fifteen minutes, I turned back and forth, from the front door to Rocky, over and over.

"What the hell is wrong with you?" Uncle Jake said. "You've got *shpilkes*?"

I settled down and faced him. "*Shpilkes*?"

"Sit still," he insisted. "How can I read the paper when you're jumping around like you've got ants in your pants?"

"Oh."

As you can tell, Uncle Jake had grown a lot more comfortable around me. That's not to say he was any less wonderful than he was the week before, but he had reverted to some of his old habits, one of which was reading the sports page during dinner.

"You've got to have a little faith," he said, reading the statistics page. "A few years ago the Mets couldn't win to save their lives. They were such bums . . . and this year, the best record in the National League."

"They must have great hitters."

Uncle Jake chewed a mouthful of roasted chicken. *"Feh,"* he said, followed by the familiar wave of his hand. "The hitting is mediocre; only one man in the starting lineup hits over three hundred. I know I go on and on about the great hitters, but when you think about it, how many were there really? You can count the great ones on your fingers. No, pitching is what wins the game, pitching and a smart coach. This year the Mets have them both. Gil Hodges has *seychel*. You understand *seychel*? It means common sense. He understands how to put runs on the board and how to win a game."

I had been reading the sports page all week long and was certainly capable of having an intelligent conversation on the subject. Somehow, though, with Rocky's eyes twinkling in the background, intelligent thought was impossible. It was as if my head was filled with that damn Los Angeles smog that Uncle Jake complained about all the time. Anyway, I saw Rocky's eyes light up even brighter than usual. I didn't have to turn around to know that the rabbi had arrived. The noise level in Kalinsky's rose precipitously, and I could hear him greet his congregants in his familiar, soothing voice.

It was only a moment before the rabbi arrived at his table. Rocky reached up and kissed him on the cheek. "Hi, Daddy," she said in a happy voice. "Hurry up. The food will be out in a minute."

Esther stood and kissed him too. "Hurry, wash your hands so we can eat. I'm starving."

"Me too," the rabbi added. "The aroma in this place . . . *oy*, I'm so hungry I could *platz*."

"I'll be right back," I told Uncle Jake.

"What's with you tonight?" he said, looking up from his newspaper. "You can't sit still?"

"I've got to go to the bathroom," I whispered.

Uncle Jake tore a piece of meat from the chicken with his fork. He plunged it into his mouth and spoke as he chewed. "Good. Go take a pish. Maybe you'll settle down."

I dashed from my seat, Rocky's piercing eyes were fixed on me as I hurried past her booth. I smiled at her. She smiled back. For some reason, she seemed intrigued with me. Her expression said, "Where the hell are you going?"

I hit the men's room just seconds after the rabbi. The door swung shut behind me. It looked like the restroom was empty, but then I heard the rabbi peeing in one of the stalls. I waited patiently for the sound of the flush and then called out, "Rabbi?"

He didn't answer immediately. I guess he was caught off guard. "Who's that?" he said.

"It's me, Rabbi, Josh, Jacob Stern's nephew."

"Ah," he said with recognition. Then I heard him zip. The stall door opened a moment later. The rabbi stepped out, adjusting his belt. He seemed very surprised. "I see you've found my private office. So, you're in the habit of cornering the clergy in the toilet?" I shook my head furiously. The rabbi smiled. "What can I do for you, Joshua Stern?"

I suddenly felt terribly silly for having trapped him in the men's room. "Is this okay?" I asked. "I didn't know where else I could speak to you."

He held his hands out with the palms upturned, looking at me like the foolish lad that I was. "In *shul?*" An awkward moment passed and then, *"New?* What can I do for you, Joshua?"

"I was wondering if you'd be able to give me bar mitzvah lessons?"

The rabbi's eyes widened. "Bar mitzvah lessons?" He pursed his lips and rocked his head side to side. After a moment, he walked to the sink and rolled up his cuffs. "How far along are you?"

I considered his question. It sounded like something a husband might ask his wife after hearing the big news. "Pardon?"

The rabbi was praying. He had filled a glass with water and was pouring it over his hands as he prayed. I waited for him to finish. "How far along, Joshua?" he said impatiently. "Have you learned your *Haftarah* yet?"

"No."

"No?"

"Honestly, I haven't learned anything yet. My parents haven't pushed me to do it."

"Ay." The rabbi seemed surprised. He wiped his hands and began rolling down his cuffs. "And when is your thirteenth birthday?"

"August the sixteenth, Rabbi."

The rabbi seemed stunned. His head was rocking from side to side again. "You mean to tell me that your father, Robert Stern, does not observe? I witnessed his bar mitzvah myself. He was a fine student of the Talmud." I shook my head sadly. *"Ay yi yi."*

My sad face must have gotten to him. I could see his expression turn from shock to sympathy. He took a step closer and patted my cheek. "Listen, Joshua, I'm starving now. You come to see me on Thursday, and we'll make a *mitzvah*. I'd see you sooner, but I have business with my family all week. This is all right by you?"

"Yes, Rabbi. Thanks."

"You're welcome, young Joshua. See you on Thursday." We shook hands. "Don't worry, Joshua," he said. "Everything will be all right." He opened the door, but then turned back and smiled. "Not here, Joshua. You come to the *shul*, ya?"

I smiled sheepishly but said nothing. The rabbi left me alone in the solitude of the men's room to ponder the monumental decision I had just made. I felt kind of proud of myself for having taken such a bold step on my own.

I decided to pee before leaving. Everything was going fine until my penis began sending me those evil signals again. "You took me out, Rocky's not more than twenty feet away in the dining room, and she looks hot. Get to it!" It was a strong argument, but I felt funny amusing myself with the same hand I had just used to shake hands with the rabbi. I considered using my left hand. After all, I was ambidextrous. It just seemed wrong. So I washed my hands and left.

~~~

"Why are you following my father into the bathroom?" Rocky demanded. She had cornered me in the long alcove that led to the restrooms. We were alone, isolated from the other diners by the extreme length of the corridor. She was glaring at me, intent on getting an answer to her question. "I asked you a question, surfer boy. What's your business with my father?"

It felt so good to be around her. The demanding way in which she spoke seemed unimportant. "How do you know I was talking to him?"

"He told me as soon as he sat down at the table."

"Oh, I asked your father to prepare me for my bar mitzvah."

"You what?" Rocky's mouth was agape, her glistening, lipstick-clad lips shining in the corridor light. "Why?"

I never seemed to be able to answer her. "Because."

"That's not an answer, surfer boy. Anyway, it won't make you a man. I want to know what your—" I could see the exact moment the revelation hit her. "Oh. I put the fear of God into you, didn't I? You think you'll stay a boy forever."

"That's not it."

"Sure it is. You're afraid you'll stay a boy. That's it, isn't it?"

She wasn't even close. It's true that she had awoken in me a sense of obligation that I had long been unaware of, but as far as a bar mitzvah bringing about physical changes in my equipment, I wasn't buying her line of tradition-steeped voodoo. All of a sudden, though, I knew just what to say to her. "You know, Rocky, for a refined girl, you're not very nice and . . . and you've got a dirty mouth." *Oh—my—God, I couldn't believe I had just said that to her.* I turned away quickly and left her standing frozen in the alcove, but I saw her expression before I left, and it was worth a million bucks.

I had definitely won that round. It was the first time I had ever stood up to her. God knows it had taken all the courage I possessed.

CHAPTER NINE

It took forever for Thursday to arrive. Uncle Jake was thrilled when he learned that I wanted to talk to the rabbi. He said that he needed to go to Manhattan anyway and was glad that I had something to do. I had met this neighborhood kid named Joe Simon and had plans to hang out with him later on in the afternoon.

The rabbi's office was small. It was cluttered with books and mail. I was waiting patiently for the rabbi to arrive when I heard someone at the door. I turned around. It was Rocky. I smiled instinctively, but quickly remembered the note we had finished on the other night. I quickly wiped the smile from my face.

This was the first time I had seen her dressed casually. She was wearing navy shorts and a white tee shirt that read: STAFF, OCEAN PARKWAY JEWISH CENTER. Her tee shirt was snugly tucked into her shorts, which made her big boobs look even bigger. I was praying that she had left her rapier wit at home, for I was sure to be putty in her hands. "You're a counselor?" I said. I expected her to say, "Obviously, surfer boy", but she didn't.

"I owe you an apology. You're a guest in our community, and I've been treating you like a virus. I'm sorry."

I had been called worse, and the idea of Rocky apologizing to me for anything . . . well, hell, I'd take as much as I could get. "Thank you," I said, but what I meant was, *would you please take off your shirt*?

"Well, that's it," she said. "I have to get back to my group. I hope I didn't upset you too much." She put her head down, turned, and began walking away.

I called to her, "Thank you, Rocky." She turned and gave me the most incredible smile, the kind that opens the doors to all kinds of possibilities. It set me on fire.

I began to smolder. Fortunately, the rabbi came right in, which extinguished the blaze quickly.

The rabbi sat down behind his desk and wiped his mouth with a napkin. "You should have come a few minutes earlier, Joshua. We could have had lunch together." He threw his napkin in the trash pail and got comfortable in his chair. He looked at me with a pleasant yet professional expression. "Joshua, I've been away from the *shul* for the past few days, which gave me the opportunity to meditate on your situation. I have an idea."

I prepared myself for the worst.

"It would be impossible for me to prepare you for your bar mitzvah in such a short time, and so I'm going to tell you something I've never told any prospective bar mitzvah before." The rabbi looked at me with wide eyes. He sighed and then stood up and closed the door to his office. "You don't mind?" he said, referring to the office door.

I shook my head. "No."

"Good." He walked around to his desk and sat down again. "I tell you this out of deference to your Uncle Jacob, who has been a member of my congregation for a long time as well as being my good friend. So listen carefully, all right, Joshua?"

I nodded eagerly. The rabbi leaned forward in his chair. "Upon attaining the age of thirteen, a Jewish boy automatically becomes a bar mitzvah. That is to say, he becomes a man in the eyes of the Jewish community. No ceremonies are needed to confer this right of passage." He paused. His eyes widened even further in an effort to convey the importance of his message. "The popular bar mitzvah ceremony is not a requirement. It does not fulfill any commandment. It is a relatively modern innovation, which is never once mentioned in the Talmud. The elaborate ceremonies and receptions everyone associates with a bar mitzvah are a modern convention, unheard of as recently as a century ago."

No shit. I was so amazed by the rabbi's honesty that I may have stopped breathing for a moment.

"I know from talking to your uncle that you're a good boy, and it's much more important to me that you become a good Jew in your heart than in your head. So what I would like to do is meet with you once a week so that I can teach you about your Jewish heritage. You're a Jew, Joshua, and the namesake of one of the most important figures in our history. You owe it to yourself to be aware of what it means to be a Jew." He settled back in his chair. "This is acceptable to you?"

"Definitely."

"Good. I have two conditions. First, you tell your uncle what we've discussed, and second, this special offer is never to be mentioned to anyone but your uncle and your parents." He held out his hand. "We have an agreement?"

I grabbed his hand and shook it thankfully. "Thank you, Rabbi."

"Good," he said. "Then it's settled. I'll see you next week. Come in time for lunch."

Just then, the rabbi's secretary appeared at the door. "Excuse me, Rabbi, Sloan-Kettering is on the line for you."

I saw the rabbi's buoyant smile disappear. "*Oy*," he sighed. I could see his spirits sink. He turned back to me. "Please excuse me, Joshua."

I stood immediately. "Thank you again, Rabbi."

I was walking on air when I left the temple. After all, I was going to be a bar mitzvah and without so much as having to memorize one syllable of Hebrew. I was looking forward to my sessions with the rabbi and learning about my faith. I was also excited because I would be around Rocky.

As I looked up the block toward Uncle Jake's apartment building, the sun peeked through the clouds in an unusual yet familiar way. It almost looked like an illustration from a nursery tale book my mom used to read from when I was little. And why not? I was in Brooklyn, a place where magic was possible.

CHAPTER TEN

Joe Simon was an urchin in every conceivable sense of the word, a child neglected by his parents and too weird to be accepted by the kids in the neighborhood. He was unusual in many respects. Physically, he was short and round, with pale, white skin, red zits, and pockmarks that stood out on his face like craters on the surface of the moon. Typical summer attire consisted of a white wife-beater stretched out over his belly, khaki shorts, and black combat boots. He never tied the laces. The tattered ends dragged on the ground and followed him everywhere. He was sitting on the stoop in front of Uncle Jake's apartment building, waiting for me as I walked up the block.

"You're late, Stern," he said. "I almost fried to death waiting for you." He glanced down at my sneakers. "Cool shoes. Where'd you get em?"

"Back home. They're the same ones Dave DeBusschere wears."

The sun was behind me. Joe squinted as he looked up. "Who?"

"Dave DeBusschere, the Knicks starting forward."

"Oh."

"I'm sure you can get them here too."

"How much?"

"About thirty dollars, I think."

"For sneakers? Are you crazy?" Joe stood up and liberated a wedgie from the crack of his butt. "What do you want to do?"

I shrugged. "I heard about this place Buzz-a-rama on Church Avenue where you can race slot cars."

"That's for nerds. Why don't we go down my basement? I've got lots of cool stuff down there."

"Your basement?"

"Yeah. Want to make explosives?" Joe was grinning like a mad scientist. I told you he was weird. "I just got a shipment from the lab supply company."

"What are you talking about? How can you make explosives?"

"Just small stuff," he advised. "Stuff like ash cans and M-80s."

"Seriously?"

"Yeah. Come on. Let's go."

Joe's mom was the superintendent of the apartment house around the corner and, as such, Joe had access to the basement. It was dark and smelled like cat pee, but at least it was cool.

I had a chemistry set back home. I was more than capable of turning a blue solution to red, growing crystals, and even lighting an alcohol lamp under my parent's careful scrutiny. Joe's lab looked like something straight out of a mad-scientist movie. A long table was filled with flasks and test tubes. Huge commercial bottles of chemicals lined the shelves above the table. I read some of the labels: nitric acid, sulfuric acid, and potassium nitrate—the kind of supplies I always wanted but knew I would never get.

"Holy shit, Joe. Where'd you get all this stuff?"

Joe locked the basement door and then joined me at his worktable. "I order it from a laboratory supply catalogue."

My mouth dropped. "Your parents let you have this stuff?"

"Sure. They give me everything I want. I write up the orders, and my dad signs them. My parents don't give a shit what I do as long as I stay out of their way."

I really didn't know how to respond to him, except to say, "You've got some incredible stuff here."

"Thanks. You into bombs or rockets?"

It wasn't the kind of question I was routinely asked. "Rockets, I think."

"Ooo," he said excitedly. "I've got some balsawood gliders." He walked over to a pile of old clothing on the floor and pulled the cardboard tube from a pants hanger. "We can stuff these with flash powder, turn the gliders into jets, and chuck them off the roof." Joe's eyes were gleaming with excitement.

"We'll get in trouble."

"Ah screw it," he said. "My parents don't give a shit."

I shrugged. We got busy making rocket-powered gliders.

We took our prototype to the roof of Uncle Jake's building. There were four six-story apartment houses on Uncle Jake's block, and their roofs ran contiguously from one corner of the block to the other, one massive expanse of rooftop. I glanced across the street at the shorter four-story apartment houses. Joe and I looked out over the roof's ledge.

"This'll be great," Joe said. "You got the matches?"

"I've got a bad feeling about this."

"Ah, you worry too much. Are all you California kids such chicken shits?"

Chicken shit, am I? I handed him the matches. "Here. I'll hold the glider. You light it."

Joe lit the glider immediately. I waited until sparks started to shoot from the engine and then heaved it off the roof. The plane soared into the sky.

"*Cool,*" Joe said gleefully. No sooner had he spoken than the glider's engine sputtered, and the rocket went into a nosedive. "Oh shit," Joe said. His face was animated with fear. A cop car had just come up the block. The glider swooped down, went in the driver-side window and came out the passenger window. The cop car jerked to a halt. I saw the driver pointing toward us. The glider's engine re-ignited, pushing the glider into a ninety-degree climb right up the face of the four-story building on the other side of the street.

"Run!" Joe yelled. "Go, go."

Joe obviously had experience avoiding the police. I followed him from one roof to the next, to the next, and then down the staircase to the rear courtyard. My heart was thumping like a kettledrum. I looked back but didn't see anything. "Where are we going?" I yelled.

"Hurry. Follow me." Joe even ran funny, sort of like Curly from *The Three Stooges*, but he was fast when chased. He ran down the length of the courtyard and leaped to the top of a three-foot concrete ledge in one quick bound. From there, he went through an opening in a wooden fence and toward his basement.

I looked through the spaces in the wooden fence, back to where we had emerged into the rear courtyard. There was no sign of the police. I sighed thankfully and ducked into Joe's basement.

"That was close," he said.

I stopped to catch my breath. When I looked at Joe, he was grinning. We broke up and laughed until it hurt.

"Did you see the look on that cop's face when the glider shot past his nose?" Joe asked. More laughter, serious laughter—the kind of laughter you're only capable of in your youth.

"Be right back," Joe told me. He disappeared into a darkened room and returned with a small, fabric-wrapped object in his hand.

"What's that?" I asked while he unwrapped it.

"You smoke hash, don't you?"

I almost choked. *"No."*

"You're kidding. Everyone does." He unwrapped the hash pipe and shoved it in my face. "I figured all the kids in LA were doing drugs."

No. Not everyone. Not me. "What do you need it for?"

Joe was already stuffing some of the hash into the pipe. He rattled off a convincing dissertation, "My mother's a drunk. She has a pint of Jim Beam before lunch and picks up from there. She shacks up with the colored super from down the block, and my dad's boffing anyone he can get his hands on. Any more questions?"

I guess not. Joe sat down in a raggedy old recliner and began sucking down the white smoke.

"You're gonna take a drag," he coughed, "aren't you?" I shook my head. "Come on, just one short drag."

To this day, I still don't know why I did it. It might have been the euphoria of knowing that I was going to become a man come hell or high water, or perhaps the adrenaline-charged escape from New York's finest. No matter, I took one quick puff and proceeded to cough my guts up. I was still coughing when we heard an ominous rapping on the cellar door.

Joe jumped out of his chair as if he had been hit with a cattle prod. He frantically tried to wave away the smoke. He picked up a pile of tattered clothes from the floor and stashed the smoking hash pipe under it.

"Joseph?" There was more rapping on the door. "Joseph, are you in there?" The voice at the door was a man's voice, an unhappy voice.

Joe ran to the door and opened it a crack, barely enough to see through. "Yes, Dad?" Joe was good at pretending to be innocent, but I saw his father's eyes probing suspiciously into the basement's recesses, looking right at me.

"What are you doing?" Joe's father asked. He sniffed the air.

"Just hanging out, Dad."

A terrifying moment passed. I could see that he was suspicious. "What have you been burning?" he asked.

"We were doing the thermite experiment. The burning metal stinks," Joe told him.

"Burning metal, huh?" Joe's father said in a doubtful manner. He stood there so long, I thought I would pee my pants. "Your supper is ready," he said and then finally turned away.

Joe relocked the door. "I have to go eat."

I watched him walk toward me. It seemed like he was walking in slow motion. His face looked blurry in the darkness.

I saw him examining my eyes. He smiled. "You're stoned, man." He put the tips of his pointer fingers and thumbs together and looked at me through the circle he had just formed. "Your pupils are this big," he said, laughing and holding the circle in front of my face for me to see.

Then he offered me some sage wisdom, "Be careful going home."

CHAPTER ELEVEN

I sat on the floor outside Joe's locked cellar door for a long while. I didn't feel stoned anymore, but wanted to make sure my pupils weren't dilated before going home. My clothes reeked from hash smoke. I would have to take a quick shower and change my clothes as soon as I hit Uncle Jake's apartment. The wind picked up, and the sky began to darken. It was too early for nightfall; a thunderstorm was coming.

I felt okay walking, just a little unsteady. I was on the corner, no more than a couple hundred feet from the entrance to Uncle Jake's apartment house when I felt the plunk of a raindrop on my shoulder. A few large drops splattered on the hot, white, concrete sidewalk in front of me, and then without warning, the sky opened up and it was teaming.

Steam rose from the sidewalk. My head began to throb the moment I began to run. I almost tripped, but recovered. I banged into the wrought-iron bars, which were overlaid on the glass entranceway doors, with my shoulder and stumbled into the empty hallway, soaked from head to toe.

I heard the rushed padding of feet approaching, sloshing through the rain, just as the door swung closed. I turned back toward the door to see Rocky's face pressed up against the glass, dripping, smiling, and looking at me in a way I really didn't understand.

She pushed the door open and walked up to me. There was something inexplicable in her smile. I was still a little fuzzy from the hash. "I need you, surfer boy," she said, her smile growing playful.

"For what?" I said.

She nuzzled my cheek. "I need you, Joshua."

We heard another set of footsteps approaching. "Hide me," she said frantically. "We can't be seen together like this."

My head was beginning to clear. The only way to go was up. "The door to the roof is open." I knew this firsthand from my recent escape from the police.

"The roof?" she said with uncertainty. Someone was about to intrude on us.

"Okay," she said. "Hurry."

The heavy door on the roof swung closed behind us. All I could think about on the way up the stairs was the wonderful news her father had given me that morning, the news I had sworn I'd only reveal to my family. Certainly though, Rocky was exempt from such restrictions. I was so excited that I blurted it out as soon as I caught my breath. "Your father said I'll automatically become a bar mitzvah the moment I turn thirteen."

Rocky grinned at me. "He's wrong." Her wet hair was back in a ponytail. She pulled the clip from it and swung her head. "I'm the only one who can make you a man." She approached me again. I was both excited and confused at the same time.

Rocky kissed me delicately on the cheek. Her lips felt warm and tender against my wet face. I was so overwhelmed that I thought I would melt. "I knew it would be you the second I woke you in the synagogue." She pressed her forehead against mine and closed her eyes. I did the same.

"I didn't even think you liked me."

"I was testing you. I had to be sure you were strong. That's why I was so tough on you. I had to be sure my reputation was safe. I would never dishonor my parents."

The rain was coming down as I imagine it had in biblical times, the days of Noah's Ark. I could feel the rain soaking through my thirty-dollar sneakers. I didn't care. It was the most perfect moment I had ever known. I would have stood there forever if she wanted to, but in the next instant, I sensed that something was wrong.

"This isn't me." She stepped back and looked off into the distance. When she turned back, her smile was gone. "You *have to* complete me." It wasn't what she had said but more the way she said it, almost pleading with me. And then among all the raindrops, I spotted the one droplet that was a tear.

"Why are you crying?" I asked.

She wiped her cheek, and I knew I had been right. In the next second, she collapsed in my arms, crying like a baby. "It's all right," I told her. "Whatever it is, it's all right."

"I'm cold," she said. "Can we get out of the rain?"

"Sure," I nodded, more confused than ever. She felt so heavy as she leaned against me, as if she had no strength of her own.

I walked her back inside.

The stairwell was cold. Wind was whistling through the hallway window. I shut the window and sat down next to her. I put my arm around her and wiped the rain from her face with my free hand. "What's wrong?"

I could see her throat tighten. "I'm really sick, Josh."

I felt an ache in my chest. It seemed like my heart had stopped beating. *Don't cry,* I told myself. *Don't you dare cry.* "What do you mean?"

"I've got acute leukemia." I must have stiffened reflexively. "Don't worry," she said. "It's not contagious."

"I wasn't—"

"It's all right, Josh. It creeps me out too."

"Well, you'll get help. I was really sick once and—"

Rocky's face became grief stricken. "Do you know what leukemia is, Josh? It's cancer."

"How do you know?"

Rocky reached into her pocket and pulled out a rain-soaked tissue. She wiped her nose and then blew it, emitting a loud honk. "Very attractive, huh?"

"You look fine."

"I've got all these symptoms. At first the doctors thought it was some kind of flu or something, but it didn't go away. I've been seeing a doctor at Sloan-Kettering. They ran some tests that confirmed it."

I felt chills all over. *Dear God.* I suddenly remembered that I was there in his office when the rabbi got the call from the hospital just that morning. "Can't they do anything for you?"

"Maybe . . . but they're going to make me feel even sicker than I feel now." Rocky turned to me. There was such intense sadness in her beautiful eyes that I couldn't help myself anymore. I started to weep.

"Don't cry, Josh," she said, stroking my cheek. "I know I've got no right to ask this of you, but you have to be strong for me. Can you do that?"

All the bar mitzvah talk had been bullshit. I wasn't a man. I really wasn't even sure what cancer was. I just knew that it was bad. I shrugged. How on earth could I help her? I was just a kid, who believed he would miraculously turn into a man on the day of his thirteenth birthday.

"I know I'm right about you. I know you'll help me," she said.

"Me? What can I do?"

Rocky wet her lips before she spoke. "I don't want to die as a girl. I want to die as a woman."

"You're talking crazy. You're not going to die."

"Just listen to me, Josh," she pleaded.

"I don't understand. You're already—"

"A bat mitzvah?" I nodded. She began to cry again. "I'm a woman before God, but not in my heart, not where it counts the most. Promise you'll help me."

"But how?"

"By coming to me when I call for you."

"Of course I'll come to you." I would do anything for her. I guess she knew that already.

"Good. Now take a good look at me. I want you to remember me the way I am now." She put her arms around me and began sobbing on my shoulder. She was inconsolable.

"Why . . . why you're beautiful, the most beautiful girl I know."

She lifted her head slowly and wiped her eyes. She managed a sad smile, just for a moment, and then it was gone. "Just promise me. Promise me that you'll come when I call."

"I . . . I—"

Rocky put her hand over my mouth. "Shhhhsh. I'll be fourteen soon. They wanted to start treatments right away, but I told them I wouldn't start until after my birthday." She rubbed my cheek, and then she stood up. She wiped her eyes and forced herself to smile. "Promise you'll remember me the way I look now."

"I promise, but I don't understand."

"You will." She was choking back tears again. Wait for my call . . . and Josh, don't tell anyone," she said and then turned to leave.

"Wait. I'll—" But she was gone and I was alone again: alone in Brooklyn and alone in my heart. And on that day, in that special place, I had received the most wonderful news I had ever gotten in my life, and I had received the worst.

CHAPTER TWELVE

"**J**oshua. *Oy vey*. Look at you. Where were you?" Uncle Jake was leaning out of the kitchen with the telephone in his hand. He looked terrible. He spoke into the phone, "He's here. He's all right. One minute." He covered the receiver with his hand. "My God. What happened to you? You're soaked. It's your parents; they're calling from London. Take the phone. I'll get you a towel."

Uncle Jake handed me the phone and dragged a chair over for me to sit on. "Hello."

"Hi, Josh, it's Dad. We're in London. How are you?"

Dear God, how was I? I was alive, breathing, confused, sad, and shocked all at once. "I'm okay, Dad. How's the trip?"

"London's great. Where were you, Sport? Your uncle was worried sick."

"I got caught in a downpour. I had to wait it out before I could come home."

"Are you sure you're okay?"

"I guess so."

"Who were you with?"

"This kid, Joe Simon."

"Simon? I don't think I know that family."

"Dad, you haven't lived in Brooklyn for more than twenty years. Do you really expect to know everyone? He's the super's kid from around the corner."

"Meg Simon? The cat lady?"

I recalled the overwhelming fragrance of cat pee in Joe's cellar. "Maybe."

Uncle Jake rushed over to me with a big bath towel. "Dry yourself," he instructed. He was carrying my pajamas in his other hand. "Get out of those wet clothes. Don't worry, I won't look."

I began drying my hair. "Thanks, Uncle Jake."

"It's a good thing I did all your laundry today. You were down to your last pair of socks."

Oh crap. I covered my face to hide my embarrassment. I hope he didn't look into my laundry bag before he dumped everything into the wash. I had planned to do the laundry myself. Anyway, Uncle Jake disappeared, leaving me to change as I talked with my dad. My feet were squishing in my thirty-dollar sneakers.

"Your mom's having her hair done. I figured I'd sneak in a surprise call to my boy. Hey, Sport, I finally had a proper afternoon tea, crumpets and all."

I tried slipping off my shirt, but I couldn't do it without putting down the phone, so I stopped because I didn't want to be rude to my dad. Thank God he had made the move across the English Channel, away from those damn, easily mispronounced bakery items. "How were they?"

"A little dry for my taste. I prefer *croy-sense*."

Those damn French breads are going to haunt me until I die. "Hey, Dad, do you have any connections in New York? It's my friend's birthday soon, and I was wondering if you could get tickets to a movie screening or something."

"Who's your friend," he asked with much interest, "the Simon kid?"

"No, just some girl I met."

"*Oh,* I see." I could almost feel him smiling on the other end of the line. "Okay. I'll make a few calls and see what I can do. They have opening nights in New York all the time. How many seats do you need?"

"I'm thinking five. I'd want to take Uncle Jake and her parents too."

"That's a very nice thing to do. I'm glad you've made such a good friend."

My dad had no idea what he had said, but his words cut right through me. All I could think of was Rocky, sitting next to me on the stairs, soaking wet, and crying on my shoulder. My throat started to ache. "Hey, Dad, I'm starting to shiver. Do you think we could talk tomorrow when Mom's around?"

"Sure, Sport. Go dry off. We'll call back tomorrow."

"Bye, Dad. Say hello to Mom."

"Will do, Sport. Bye."

I thought about Joe Simon, hiding out in his cellar, smoking hash to keep from letting his rotten parents drive him off the deep end. I wasn't big on the L word, but I just had to say it. "I love you, Dad."

My dad said it too. I hung up and rushed into the bathroom before Uncle Jake could see that I was crying.

CHAPTER THIRTEEN

On the following Thursday, I arrived at the temple early enough to join the rabbi for lunch. I found him at a folding table with Rocky and his wife at the far end of a dining hall, which was filled with campers. I walked over to the table and waited for the rabbi's invitation to sit. Rocky smiled at me knowingly. The rabbi stood. "Joshua, please join us. We're just getting started."

"Hello, Joshua. Enjoying your vacation?" Esther asked. Her eyes were still mired in sadness. Now I understood why.

I replied, "Yes, thank you. Brooklyn is a lot different than California." Rocky giggled.

The rabbi looked at her. "Something's funny?" he asked with a big smile. Rocky shrugged and glanced at me quickly. I felt so close to her that I wanted to throw my arms around her and hold her. The rabbi turned to me. "In what way, Joshua? How is Brooklyn different?"

I thought for a moment. "The people," I replied.

"People are people," the rabbi replied. "Los Angeles, Brooklyn, what's the difference?"

"The people here are warmer," I said.

The rabbi looked at his wife and then smiled at me affectionately. "Warmer? This I will accept. We live in a wonderful community, everyone feels for one another. Dig in, Joshua. The food here is simple, but it's homemade."

The rabbi went on and on over lunch about the Jewish community and how proud he was to be the rabbi for such a fine group of people. All the while, Rocky and I mastered the art of secretive eye contact. The rabbi and his wife were so engrossed in the meal that they hardly noticed.

They served Good Humor pops for dessert. I was finished with my pop before I got up the guts to make my announcement. I waited until the rabbi had poured his non-dairy creamer into his coffee. "Rabbi, do you like westerns?"

The rabbi looked up from his steaming cup of coffee. "Westerns, you mean cowboys and indians? Why sure. Why do you ask, Joshua?"

"We . . . I mean, my family and I would like to invite you to a screening of *True Grit*. It's a new western starring John Wayne. It's our way of thanking you for your generosity." I watched Rocky for her reaction. Her electric-green eyes were sizzling once more.

The rabbi's eyes widened. "Generosity? What generosity? Where, not in California?"

"In New York. The studio will send a car to pick us all up, Uncle Jake too."

He turned to Rocky and Esther. "*New, girls,* you'd like to go?" They both nodded eagerly. He turned back to me. "Thank you, Joshua, but this is completely unnecessary. All right . . . When?"

"Sunday evening."

"I think we're free, no?" he asked Esther.

Esther wiped her mouth with her napkin. "Such a generous offer." Her eyes connected with mine, and in that moment, I think she understood that I knew about Rocky. Only a mother could know. She smiled at me sweetly. "Yes, we're free, Josef."

"It would be an honor, Joshua. Thank you. We'll use the occasion to celebrate my lovely daughter's fourteenth birthday." He blew Rocky a kiss and then leaned over and patted me on the cheek. "This is not a surprise from Joshua, the one who led the Jewish people to freedom. This is what I'll teach you on your first lesson: the campaigns of Joshua."

Rocky seemed alive again, the way I wanted her to look, the way she deserved to look. I was so happy about the way they had reacted that, to use a Yiddish word I had recently mastered, I was ready to *platz*.

CHAPTER FOURTEEN

I preferred Rocky in her tee shirt and shorts, but I had to admit that she looked great in the pink dress she wore to the screening. She was wearing more makeup than I had seen her wear before. She was so pretty that it took my breath away.

Uncle Jake and the rabbi got into the front seat next to the driver in the Cadillac that the studio's New York office had sent to pick us up. I thought that Esther would insist on sitting between Rocky and me, but she didn't, and I was happy when she got into the back seat and slid over to the end. Rocky's dress was cut above the knee, and it rode up her leg when she squeezed in and shut the door. We sat next to one another, close enough for me to feel the warmth of her body through the sheer fabric of her dress. Esther kept a watchful eye on us, but there was no way that she could sense the way I felt.

I hated westerns, but the adults seemed to be very entertained by it. Rocky and I spent the time trying to look into each other's eyes, ignoring the horse chases and shooting, looking at the screen only when we thought the adults were getting suspicious. The theater was very dark, and I even managed to rest my hand on hers for part of the time.

About halfway through, Rocky leaned over and whispered in my ear, "Forget about how I looked the other day. I want you to remember the two of us exactly the way we are right now." She rested her forehead against my temple for an instant, and I felt her softness and warmth. For one brief, indescribable moment, I was in heaven.

Our driver had been instructed to take us home after the screening, but the rabbi was so thrilled about the special outing that he insisted we take the subway to Junior's for cheesecake. "*New*, you've ridden the subway, Joshua?"

"Just once," I replied. "When I went to the museum with Uncle Jake."

"This is the way to travel in New York. It's okay with you?" I nodded.

"Good, then we go." He turned to Uncle Jake. "Jakela, tell your nephew about Junior's cheesecake."

"Cheesecake like this you can't get in your cockamamie California, Josh. It's the water, Josh; no one's got water like Brooklyn."

This was a real shocker. Now, my mom bakes all the time. She makes a killer cheesecake, and I know for a fact that there's no water in her recipe, but it didn't matter. We could have been visiting Ashtabula for all I cared. The evening was being extended, which meant more time with Rocky. It was the only thing that mattered.

The subway ride was a hoot. It rocked and creaked like a Disneyland amusement ride. We all sat on one long bench; Rocky and I were at the end. The lights would go out every few minutes, and when they did, Rocky and I would steal glances of one another through the darkness, feeling alone and intimate. Bathed in the darkness, it was almost as if we had the entire car to ourselves.

Junior's cheesecake was every bit as good as they had said. I wolfed down a slice of strawberry cheesecake, but Rocky barely picked at hers. I wondered if her poor appetite was due to her having cancer. Suddenly, I was fighting back tears again.

"Le'Chaim." I looked up. The rabbi was offering a toast. We all raised our teacups. "Look at them," the rabbi said. "Two beautiful, young people. May they—"

"Excuse me," Esther said as she jumped from her seat. She rushed from the table. I could see that she was crying as she made her way to the restroom.

The rabbi patted me on the leg. "Don't worry, Joshua. She gets very emotional. She's okay. Boy, that John Wayne . . . he's some cowboy, no?" he said, trying to change the subject. I nodded and then turned away. I caught his sad, knowing glance at Rocky from the corner of my eye.

CHAPTER FIFTEEN

The rabbi and I had lunch again, but when I asked where Rocky and Esther were, he replied that they had some business to attend to.

Rocky's call came the very next day.

"It's time, surfer boy." Surfer boy was no longer meant in a derogatory sense. It was now a term of endearment, and I smiled at her words. "Can you get out of going to temple tomorrow?" That underlying sense of urgency was back in her voice.

"Why?"

"Because, Josh . . . because there might not be another time."

"The summer's only half over."

"Please, Josh, try to skip services and come to my house."

"Won't your parents be— What will I tell Uncle Jake?"

"Tell him you're tired. Tell him you don't feel well. Tell him anything. Just come. You promised."

"Okay. I'll think of something."

"Thank you," she said, sounding intensely grateful. "Oh and Josh, I may look a little tired. I don't want you to be shocked when I answer the door."

"You're silly, how could I be— Oh. All right."

"I have to go. I have an appointment at the hospital this afternoon. Don't be late."

We made our customary trip to Al's barbershop that afternoon. As always, Al took a little off the top. He even found a few whiskers on my chin. He cut them off carefully and wrapped me up in a towel. It was not the happy experience I was looking forward to. Alone, hidden beneath the towel, I felt miserable. All I could think about was Rocky and the cancer that was eating her alive. I prepared for the worst. In my mind, I pictured her opening the door to her house, her face tired and so withered that I would hardly recognize it. I felt my face contort with sadness. I was glad that the towel was there to hide me.

Kelley walked into the barbershop just as we were about to leave. Uncle Jake was greeting him with his usual level of indifference, when we noticed Rocky and

Esther across the street—they were climbing the stairs to the elevated subway platform on McDonald Avenue. They didn't see us, but we got a good look at Rocky. She looked tired and weak as she ascended the steps. Her face looked drawn. I understood what she had meant on the phone.

"Shainera menchen haut me gelicht in drert." Kelley smiled at Uncle Jake. "You see," he boasted as he glanced at Rocky, "I speak a little Yiddish too."

Uncle Jake looked horrified. He took a step back and without warning thrust his huge hands forward. They exploded against Kelley's chest making a noise like a thunderclap. Kelley fell backwards, onto the floor of Al's shop. Uncle Jake stood over Kelley waving a fist and swearing. "*Nish do gedachet,* you, you good for nothing. You haven't got a shred of human decency in your entire body."

I froze. I couldn't believe the sudden, bitter rage that had erupted from my uncle.

Kelley was on the floor, reeling. "What happened?" he asked.

Al raced over to help him. "What happened, Jake? What did he say?"

Uncle Jake grabbed me by the arm and pulled me out of the store. "Tell him to sue me," he yelled back to Al. "Tell him I hope he drops dead."

CHAPTER SIXTEEN

Uncle Jake was unable to speak all the way home. He ripped open the door to his apartment and made straight for the refrigerator. A large bottle of kosher wine sat on the top shelf. He rinsed out two jelly glasses and filled one of them. Uncle Jake took a large gulp of wine and then handed me a glass. "You're thirteen soon. You're old enough for a little wine." Uncle Jake coated the bottom of the second glass and handed it to me.

"Are you okay?" I asked.

"I'm mad," he said. "I should have killed him." Uncle Jake gulped down the rest of the wine and then stormed into the living room, carrying his empty glass and the bottle of wine. He flopped down onto the couch. I followed him in and sat down on the recliner next to him.

"What did he say about Rocky?"

Uncle Jake refilled his glass. He took another sip and then looked me in the eye. "Tell the truth, Josh. You know what's going on with her?" I nodded. "I thought so. This is why you got the idea to take us all to the movies, no?" I nodded again. "You've got a big heart, Joshua Stern. Learn to guard it. You like her, no?" I looked back at him with a sheepish expression. I took a quick drink of wine. "It's all right, Josh. She's a beautiful girl." I could see him misting up. "Terrible. Just terrible."

"What did Kelley say?"

"The *putz*, so proud he was to show he spoke a little Yiddish. He probably didn't even know what it meant. He said, 'They buried nicer looking people than that.' I told him it should happen to him."

I put down the glass of wine. My head dropped into my hands.

"This is hitting you hard, I can see," Uncle Jake said.

I nodded, with my face covered by my hands. I felt Uncle Jake's hand stroke my hair.

"Look at me, Josh." I slowly lifted my head. Uncle Jake smiled at me tenderly. "This is a lot for a young man to handle. All we can do is pray."

"Does cancer kill everyone, Uncle Jake?"

"No, Josh, not everyone. I won't kid you, it's very serious, but there's always hope."

We spent the next few minutes in silence. Uncle Jake finished another glass of wine. "You really surprised me," I said.

"You mean when I shoved Kelley?"

"Yes."

"I'm sorry, Josh, I shouldn't have done that. It's just that those words, those awful words, they cut right into my heart. I know this girl since her mother carried her in her arms. That Kelley is such a fool. You know I'm not like this, don't you, Josh?"

"I know, Uncle Jake. If I understood what he had said, I would have hit him too."

Uncle Jake grinned. "Good for you." I could see the wine was getting to him. His eyes looked glassy, and he slumped back into the couch. "You'll be back home in a few weeks, and you can forget all this sadness. You can go back to your life. I'm sorry you had to know from such trouble." He looked at me with glassy eyes. He had a sad smile on his face. "It's funny, everything I love ends up in California. I'll miss you, Josh. You're a wonderful young man."

"Why don't you come back with me, Uncle Jake? We've got lots of room in our house."

He smiled warmly. "That's a lovely thing to say, but I'd be like a fish out of water. Who would give me a shave every Friday? I would miss the brisket at Kalinsky's too much. There was a time, Josh, a time I almost moved to California, believe it or not." He sighed. "But it just didn't work out and now . . . now I'm too old."

"My mom says that you're never too old."

"Your mother's not a tired old man. I was in love with a girl many years ago. Her name was Ida Rubenstein. She played on Broadway, a dancer. I used to sing to her all the time, 'Ida, sweet as apple ci—i—i—der.'" I could see that Uncle Jake was pretty drunk. "She wanted to be a movie actress and shortened her name to Ida Ruby. She begged me to go with her to California, but Etta—" He sat up. "You know about my sister, Etta?"

"No, Uncle Jake."

"You had an aunt who died many years before you were born. She was ill at the time. Your Grandpa Ted had died just a few years before. I couldn't leave her. So I let Ida go." He sighed again, a long, troubled sigh. "And I never saw her again."

"Did she become a movie actress?"

"Not that I know of, Josh. She wasn't the kind of woman to lay down on a casting couch and let the big shots *shtup* her for a bit part. No, I doubt she made it." Uncle Jake rolled over on the couch with his eyes closed. "Let that be a lesson to you," he yawned. "If you love someone, you should never let them go."

The next thing I knew, Uncle Jake was snoring so loudly, it made the furniture vibrate. I drank down the rest of my wine, hoping I would fall asleep too. There was so much to think about that my head began to hurt. God must have heard my prayers, because I felt my eyes closing, and then . . .

CHAPTER SEVENTEEN

I awoke to the sound of Uncle Jake rushing around the apartment. I opened my eyes and saw him racing past the bedroom door. I yawned. Uncle Jake bolted into the room. "My head hurts," I said. I wasn't acting, I was telling the truth.

"You're sick?" he asked

I was about to answer honestly when I remembered that I had to meet Rocky. "I feel terrible."

"Stay in bed," he told me. "There's Bayer aspirin in the medicine cabinet. *New*, you think you need to see a doctor?"

I wasn't much of a liar. "I just want to sleep."

"We both had too much wine last night. Maybe that's it. You don't mind if I run over to *shul*? You'll be all right?"

"I'm okay. I'm going back to sleep."

"I'll see you in a few hours. Feel better, Josh."

"Okay." I thought it funny that things were working out this way. I didn't even have to make up a phony excuse for not going to temple. I felt as if I was a player in a story that had been scripted by God.

I heard the door slam a little while later. I got dressed and began walking to Rocky's house. I started thinking about what was going to happen when I got there and how to react when I saw her. In a way, it was good that I had gotten a peek at her the other day so that I wouldn't be surprised when she opened the door. My headache disappeared as I walked, but I was unable to think about what was going to happen when I arrived at her house.

The door opened slowly. Rocky was hiding behind it. "Get in here before the neighbors see you," she said.

I entered quickly, and she closed the door at once. The treatments had begun to take their toll on her. Rocky's cheeks were sunken, and the area around her eyes was dark. She was wearing extra makeup, but she didn't look the way she had when we went to the screening together. The unmistakable mask of sickness was there and it could not be hidden.

Rocky stroked my cheek and then stepped back. She had a heavy cardigan sweater wrapped around her, and I could see that she had lost weight. Her hair was different too; it had lost some of its shine. She fluffed her hair. "I hope I look all right?"

"You look great."

"You're a terrible liar, Josh." She smiled and rubbed my cheek again. "I'm glad you came."

Rocky took my hand and we shuffled into the kitchen. "It's freezing in here," she said, although I didn't think the house was cold at all.

The kitchen table was arranged with two wine glasses, which were covered by a napkin. There were two gold rings on the table. I picked one of them up. "Where did you get these?" I asked.

Rocky smiled. "They're not real, Josh. I found them with some dress-up stuff I still have from when I was a little girl." She looked up at the wall clock. "My parents will come home right after services. They won't even stay for the *Kiddush* because they're afraid of leaving me alone for too long. We should hurry. Rocky pointed to one of the kitchen chairs. "Sit *mine chousin*, my groom."

Is this what she wanted? I wondered. *A child's wedding ceremony?* I was still uncertain, but I would do anything to make her happy.

"I'll say the *moatse* over the wine." Rocky said a short prayer and then uncovered the wine glasses and handed one to me. "Take a sip," she said.

I recognized the flavor of the wine from the night before. "This is the same kind my Uncle Jake keeps in the house."

"Are you ready to continue?" she asked.

I smiled. "I think so."

Rocky picked up one of the wedding bands. "Before God, are you, Joshua Stern, willing to take Rachel Tannenbaum as your bride, to have and to hold, to honor and cherish until death do us part?"

"I do."

Rocky blushed and then her eyes got wet. She began to sniffle. "Now ask me."

"Before God, are you Rachel Tannenbaum, willing to take Joshua Stern as your husband, to have and to hold, to honor and cherish until death do us part?"

"I do." Rocky handed me one of the rings and extended her ring finger. I slipped it on. She looked down at her hand. Her lips began to quiver and then a torrent of tears came forward. She raced off to the bathroom and shut the door.

My heart deflated as I listened to her sobbing in the bathroom. My head started to throb again, so badly that I needed to rest it on the table. She was in the bathroom a long while, so long that I worried about her parents coming home and finding us together.

Rocky finally emerged from the bathroom. I could see that she was struggling to continue. She made her way back to the table and put the other ring on my finger. Rocky stood and I did the same. We came face to face. "You may kiss your bride, Josh, if you still want to."

We moved closer. My heart was racing at the prospect of my first real kiss. We were just inches apart, both of us tentative and unsure of ourselves. A moment passed, and then our lips were less than an inch apart, pausing almost touching, and then I felt the gentle caress of her lips against mine, just for a second, and then we pulled apart. The fire was once again alive in Rocky's incredible green eyes. "Come with me, Josh."

She took my hand and led me up the staircase, looking back at me and smiling as we ascended. I began to tremble and prayed that she wouldn't notice.

We were in her bedroom, standing alongside the bed.

"Hold me, Josh. I'm so cold, so horribly cold." I surrounded her in my arms and could feel that she was trembling too. Rocky kissed my shoulder and then looked deeply into my eyes.

"I'm a little scared."

She stroked my cheek. "Me too." Rocky held my face in her hands, looking into my eyes. "Sweet, handsome Josh. I know it hasn't been long, but I know in my heart that I love you."

Rocky reached down and pulled the cover back from the bed. She let go of my hand and slipped under the covers, holding them up so that I could get in alongside her. "Do you love me too, Josh?" she said as she stared into my eyes.

I knew at that moment that I would never love anyone more. I got into her bed, fully dressed, and pulled the cover over us. I was scared, and afraid to confess my uncertainty, but my emotions took over. "I'm not sure what to do."

Rocky smiled at me. "Just hold me, Josh, hold me like a husband would hold his wife and make me feel like the two of us are one. That's all I want. That's all I will ever need."

She made me understand that her need was for emotional love. I put my arms around her and squeezed tightly, trying to combine the two of us into one.

CHAPTER EIGHTEEN

After that day, I wanted to be with her all the time, but that didn't happen. I didn't see her again until the following Saturday. Rocky managed to make a brief appearance at services, but she sat with her mother, and all I had of her that day were her tender glances. She only stayed a short while, and when she left, I could see by the way she walked that she was weak.

I found out from Uncle Jake that Rocky was not taking well to her treatments. I even got up the guts to call her house, but the rabbi only thanked me for my concern. He didn't put her on the phone.

Uncle Jake and I went to services the next week. I was surprised to find out that the rabbi had taken a leave of absence. I didn't ask Uncle Jake if he knew but I'm pretty sure he did.

I was sitting on the end of the bed, taking off my dress clothes after services, when Uncle Jake walked in with his hands behind his back. "Guess which one," he said.

I smiled wearily and tapped his right shoulder. My arms felt so heavy I could barely lift them.

"Correct," he announced. He brought his hand forward, showing me a pair of tickets for a Mets baseball game. "Box seats," he boasted excitedly. "How about it?"

"Sure." There was no emotion in my response. If I couldn't be with Rocky, I didn't care how I passed the time.

"Such excitement," Uncle Jake said, holding his face in his hands as he shook his head woefully. He sat down on the bed next to me. "If you don't want to go, I can find someone else who wants them. It's up to you, Josh."

I shrugged. "No, I'd like to go."

Uncle Jake began stroking the back of my head. "Do you remember what I said about having a big heart?"

"Yeah."

"You're a good, sweet boy, Josh, but you have to learn how to protect yourself. I know you care for this girl. We all do. Rachel is a wonderful child, but you have to learn to go on." He sighed. "Look at me. I buried my brother and sister within three years of one another. I thought I would follow them into the grave, but I didn't. We have to be strong, Josh. We have to go on."

"You also told me that if you love someone you should never let them go." I buried my head in my hands. I felt tears rushing forward. I fought them back because I didn't want to cry in front of him.

Uncle Jake lifted my chin. "At your age, Josh, what do you know about—" I saw the corners of his lips curl downward. He pressed his lips together until they turned white. "Oy. Forget what I just said, Josh, It's okay to cry."

CHAPTER NINETEEN

We got to Shea Stadium early enough to catch batting practice. Uncle Jake brought along his mitt, so that we could snare a foul ball if it came our way. He insisted that we have a light breakfast so that we could stuff ourselves with hotdogs at the ballpark.

"This is my favorite part, Josh, watching the ballplayers warm up. It takes me back." Uncle Jake stood up in his seat when Cleon Jones took his batting practice. "Watch Jones," he said. "He's got a beautiful swing. Watch him, Josh. Watch the way he makes contact with the ball. This is what you have to do." Uncle Jake turned to me. "Stand up and have a good look. See how relaxed he is? Watch his face—this is confidence." Uncle Jake swung an imaginary bat as he watched Jones pound baseball after baseball into the outfield. In his eyes, I could see how badly he missed the game.

I stood up to watch as Uncle Jake had instructed. He was right; from the look on Jones's face, there seemed little doubt that he would nail the ball every time. "I wish I could do that," I said.

"Only with practice, Josh. You think he was born with such confidence? It took years of hard work."

He sat down a minute later. "I wanted to get the tickets to take you on your exact birthday, but this was the best I could do. It's all right?"

"It's great, Uncle Jake." I wanted to give him a hug, but it wasn't the kind of thing I was comfortable doing in front of thousands of fans. "Thanks."

"You're welcome. So, what do you want to do on your birthday?"

I had been thinking about it all night, so the answer was already on the tip of my tongue. "I'd like to see how Rocky's doing. I thought maybe we could go over to her house and bring her some lunch."

Uncle Jake gritted his teeth. I was afraid to hear what he was going to say. "Josh, I'm afraid Rocky isn't home these days. She's in a hospital in Manhattan. I'm sorry. Maybe when she comes home."

"Can't we go to see her?" I asked beseechingly. "I'm only going to be here a couple more weeks."

Uncle Jake shrugged. His expression was one of hopelessness. "We'll see." I could see that he had nothing else to add, but I kept looking at him all the same, pleading with him to say yes. He saw me staring at him. "I'll ask the rabbi. Now please, Sweetheart, enjoy the afternoon. It's a beautiful day. Who knows the next time you'll have a chance to see a team on their way to the World Series . . . those *farshtinkener* Dodgers—" He waved a finger in the air playfully. "They're not going anywhere."

He had a gift for being able to lift my spirits. I smiled. It was almost as if he had waved a magic wand.

We had eaten two hotdogs each before the end of the third inning. The sun was overhead by then, baking us like Coney Island clams. Uncle Jake ordered drinks, a Coke for me and a beer for himself. I was reaching for my soda when I heard the crack of the bat. I caught his cup of beer in midair as it fell from Uncle Jake's hand. His hand was like lightning as it shot out and grabbed the fly ball, a foot in front of me, heading right for my face. It all happened so fast that I didn't know what he was doing until I saw the baseball in his hand. "Wow," I said. "Nice catch."

"You too," he said, reaching for the cup of beer. "Almost nothing spilled." Uncle

Jake handed me the ball. "Here, Joshua. Agee hit it. We'll see if he'll autograph it for you after the game." Uncle Jake smiled, looking as if he had done nothing at all. I shook my head in disbelief. I could only imagine how good he had been when he was young.

I felt Uncle Jake's hand on mine. He pulled my hand closer to examine it. "Where did you get that cheap ring?" he asked.

I never thought he would notice, but then it dawned on me that he had been a jeweler and was probably accustomed to looking at people's hands. "It's just a ring," I said.

"You got married since you got here?" I didn't answer. I didn't know what to tell him. "It's not real gold," he told me. "Be careful it doesn't turn your finger green."

"It won't."

He turned his attention back to the ball field. "You wouldn't want to tell me where you got that?" he asked.

"It's just a ring," I repeated.

"Okay, I won't ask again." He didn't, but I could tell from his expression that he already knew. "Wear it well, Joshua," he said. "Wear it well."

CHAPTER TWENTY

I put on my best outfit to visit the hospital. It was my first visit to a hospital of any sort, and I didn't know what to expect.

Uncle Jake walked right up to the receptionist. "We'd like to visit with a patient," Uncle Jake said. "Rachel Tannenbaum."

The receptionist thumbed through a register on the counter and then handed Uncle Jake two passes. "You can only stay an hour," she said.

"What floor is she on? Four?" Uncle Jake asked.

"No, she's on six, in the pediatric ward, room 610."

Uncle Jake smiled to show his appreciation. He put his hand on my shoulder and led me towards the elevators.

The elevator was full and stopped on every floor. Each time the elevator door opened, I read the wall directory. Each floor said something different, like *X-Ray* or *Pre-surgical Testing*. The sign on four read: *Chemotherapy.* The one on six read: *Pediatric Oncology.*

"What does oncology mean?" I whispered to Uncle Jake as we got out of the elevator.

It was about the hundredth time I had asked him a question about cancer over the last couple of days. Uncle Jake had made a valiant attempt at answering them all, but he was far from being an authority on the subject. "I think it has to do with the treatment of cancer," he said. "I'm not exactly sure."

Rocky was in a semi-private room. "You can go in first," Uncle Jake said. "I'll say hello after . . . if she feels up to it."

The door to her room was open. I peeked in. There was a girl in the first bed, sleeping. Her head was bandaged, and there were a dozen different tubes leading under her blanket. A small machine near her bed emitted a continuous beep. I was ready to walk in, but my body wouldn't move. An odd feeling came over me. I think I felt guilty about being healthy. I felt Uncle Jake's large hand on my shoulder.

"Are you sure you're up to this?" he asked.

I wasn't sure that I was, but I nodded anyway and slowly walked into the room, desperate to see Rocky, but dreading what I would find.

My sneakers, my new five-dollar Keds, were silent on the hospital floor, but the girl in the first bed began moaning as I walked by, as if she somehow sensed someone had entered the room.

Rocky was lying in bed and looking out the window. Her hair was much thinner than the last time I had seen her. It was wispy, her scalp peeking through in spots. Her skin had become an unusual tan color. It took a moment, but then something occurred to me. I looked back at Uncle Jake, who was standing in the doorway, watching me. His skin and Rocky's were almost exactly the same shade. I felt an ache in my chest. Suddenly two-and-two added up to one inescapable conclusion: his trips to Manhattan each Thursday, his cocoa-colored skin, the mad dashes to the bathroom, and the baldness. *Damn.* I felt my face contorting in misery just as Rocky turned toward me. I forced myself to smile.

Rocky's eyes flashed like small lightning bolts. She smiled as I had never seen her smile before. She held up her hand, showing me the back of her fingers and the ceremonial gold ring that she was still wearing. In the next moment, she extended her hand toward me, beckoning me closer.

"Josh," she said excitedly. She opened her arms to hug me.

There were no tubes attached to her like the other girl. I stood next to the bed for a moment, uncertain if I would disturb anything by hugging her. "It's okay," she said, waving me closer. Her arms closed around me, clutching me tightly. "I knew you'd come," she said in a deeply emotional voice. "I wish I'd known; I'd have put on some makeup."

The orbits of her eyes were still dark, but she looked better than I had expected. I noticed an IV start was taped to her arm. "You look fine," I said. "I really missed you."

"I missed you too."

"Your parents wouldn't tell me what was going on. I wasn't sure they'd let me visit. So, how are you feeling?"

"Better," she said in a jubilant voice. "I mean not *better*, but *better*. The treatments were really awful, so they've stopped them for a while, until they can figure out what else to do. I actually finished my breakfast this morning," she said proudly. Then her eyes searched my hand for my wedding band. Her face brightened even further. "Thank you," she said. She looked toward the door to see if anyone was looking. Uncle Jake had disappeared. She picked up my hand and kissed it.

"I'm glad you're okay. How long do you think they'll keep you here?" In the back of my mind, I was hoping she would be able to come home before I left for California.

Her smile dulled. "Oh, Josh, they're not even talking about sending me home. I'm not well, I'm just feeling better."

My heart sank. I had misinterpreted her enthusiasm completely. All I could say was, "Oh."

Rocky must have seen my heart sink. She touched my chin and directed my gaze back toward her. "Look at *me*," she said.

I nodded and forced a smile, but I was dying on the inside. "When you get home, I'm going to take you to Junior's for a huge piece of strawberry cheesecake."

I read the sadness in her eyes. They said, *if I come home.* Instead, she said, "I'd really like that."

"Josh." Uncle Jake's voice startled me. He was calling from the doorway, signaling to me with his finger. I could see the rabbi and his wife standing with him. I turned back to Rocky. "I think they want me to leave."

"Already?" she said with disappointment in her voice.

I shrugged. "I guess. Is it okay if I come back?"

Rocky's face brightened. "You'd better." Then she tugged on my shirt, pulling me down toward her. "I love you," she whispered.

"I love you too," I said.

I could see her getting emotional, but she recovered quickly. "Smart move," she said. "Now get out of here and make sure you don't look at any other girls on your way home."

I knew she was just kidding. All the same, I said, "I won't."

CHAPTER TWENTY-ONE

Uncle Jake went in to see Rocky, but didn't stay long. Esther went in when he came out, and the rabbi invited us to the cafeteria for coffee. He explained that he and Esther were living in an apartment near the hospital, in some kind of special facility for the families of patients at the hospital.

"The food's *drek* here," the rabbi said, "but they make a decent cup of coffee."

Uncle Jake took a sip from the paper cup. "Not bad," he said, but then added extra sugar.

The rabbi bought me an ice cream pop, which I devoured in seconds.

"So what's happening?" Uncle Jake asked the rabbi.

The rabbi glanced at me as he answered Uncle Jake. "*New*, we can talk in front of the youngster?"

Uncle Jake gave me a playful slap on the cheek. He smiled warmly. "Joshua is very interested in Rachel's condition. Please—"

"This is all right by you, Joshua?" the rabbi asked me. I nodded.

"The doctors are giving her a little time to build up her strength, then they want to try a new treatment, one that won't make her so sick."

"I'm sure they'll find something," Uncle Jake said. I looked at his cocoa-colored skin. I was pretty darn sure that he was getting treatments himself, and he seemed as healthy as a horse. It gave me hope.

"Now the search begins," the rabbi said. "They're going to start looking for a bone marrow donor, just in case the chemotherapy doesn't work."

"What's this?" Uncle Jake asked. "Some new kind of treatment?"

I listened intently to the rabbi's explanation. "You know the marrow, Jake, the inside of the bone?"

"Sure," Uncle Jake said with a nod of the head. "The soft part."

"Yes . . . I didn't know this, but that's where the body makes the blood cells. They want to give Rachel someone's healthy blood cells."

Uncle Jake plopped his bare arm on the table. *"Here,"* he offered. "Take mine."

I could see the rabbi was getting choked up. "Thank you, Jakela." The rabbi turned to me. "Your Uncle is an angel, Joshua." The rabbi's voice became hoarse. "He touches me so . . . but I'm afraid I can't take from you, my friend." He looked at Uncle Jake in a knowing way. His voice was disappearing. He took a sip of coffee to moisten his throat. "You see? I'm getting *farklempt*."

"*Oy,*" Uncle Jake said. "I—"

The rabbi cast a cautious glance in my direction.

"Ah," Uncle Jake said. He nodded in a barely perceptible manner. "I'll help you find someone. I'll spread the word."

"I wish it were so easy; donors are rare. They have to find someone with exactly the right—" The rabbi scratched his head. "What's the word they use? Oh yes, profile. First they check their records. If they don't find a match, they ask for volunteers to take a blood test. Even Esther and I don't match. I'm afraid the doctors are not optimistic . . . but I pray."

"Test my blood." The words came out of mouth automatically. "I'll bet I'm her match."

"He has your heart, Jake," the rabbi said, wiping the corner of his eye. He turned to me. "The chances are rare, Josh. So rare."

"I insist," I said to the rabbi.

"Josh, I can't let you without your parent's permission," Uncle Jake said.

"Then let's call them. I have their itinerary at home. Let's go home and call them."

Uncle Jake turned to the rabbi. "This blood test, it's a big deal?"

"No," the rabbi replied.

"So they can test Joshua too," Uncle Jake said. The rabbi nodded. Uncle Jake patted the back of my hand. "We are here now," Uncle Jake said. "You think a small white lie is in order, Josh?"

"I'm not leaving until they test me, Uncle Jake."

"I see," he replied. He turned back to the rabbi. "Rabbi, his mind is made up. There's a blessing for a small transgression like this?"

The rabbi managed a weak smile. "In Judaism, Jake, there's a blessing for everything."

Uncle Jake focused on me. "This is our secret, right, Josh? If your parents find out, they'll murder me."

I had never been a Boy Scout, but I knew the salute. I raised two fingers. "Scout's honor."

The rabbi smiled warmly. He reached out and took hold of our hands. Then he closed his eyes and blessed us in Hebrew, in words I still don't understand.

CHAPTER TWENTY-TWO

We raced home after I took my blood test. My parents were in Greece, preparing to go to dinner when we called. Uncle Jake and I crossed our fingers as we lied to them, asking for their permission to take the blood test. Uncle Jake, the old jewelry salesman, was the one that closed the deal. He said the chances of them finding a donor were worse than a million-to-one. "Why not let the boy feel good about himself? There's no harm."

Afterward, Uncle Jake poured us both a little wine. "I don't like lying to your parents, Josh, but it was for a good cause."

"I agree," I said consoling him. In my heart, I was sure I was Rocky's match.

CHAPTER TWENTY-THREE

It was the rabbi himself who told us the good news.

I believed in my heart that all of it was part of God's plan: my parent's trip to Europe, my spending the summer in Brooklyn, meeting Rocky—it was, as they say, all meant to be. The news made me feel ten feet tall.

Uncle Jake had two glasses of wine before placing the call to Greece to tell my parents the news, but they had already checked out. I pulled out their itinerary and saw that they were on their way to Sweden, and with the difference in time zones, we wouldn't be able to reach them until the next morning.

"We can't do a thing until I speak to your parents, Josh. You understand this, no?"

"We can go for the meeting with Rocky's doctor tomorrow. I don't think my parents would object to that."

Uncle Jake thought long and hard before answering. "Probably not. There's no real harm. You're sure you want to do this?"

"I've never been more sure of anything, Uncle Jake."

Uncle Jake looked at me with a warm smile. "You're a *mensch*, Josh, a wonderful gentleman. I'm so proud of you." He opened his arms to hug me, but as he stepped forward, the phone rang. "*New*, maybe it's them?"

Uncle Jake rushed into the kitchen. "Hello," he said hopefully. "*Oh.* Hello, Sweetheart. Just a minute." I could tell by his response that he was surprised. He held the phone out toward me. "It's for you, Josh." He smiled broadly as he handed me the phone.

"Hello?" I said.

"Hi, surfer boy." I was so happy to hear Rocky's voice that my knees buckled and I had to brace myself against the kitchen wall.

"I can only stay on the phone a minute. My parents just stepped out of the room."

"How are you feeling?"

"Honestly, not so good. They started my new medication today and I'm pretty nauseous . . . but I know you'll fix that. Joshua, my Joshua, you've given me so much." Rocky's voice was weak, but hopeful. "My father believes that you're one of God's miracles. He thinks you're the Joshua from the bible."

"I'm just me, Rocky. I'm just—"

"My lovely Josh. They're back. I have to go. Bye."

"Bye, Rocky." I didn't want to hear the dial tone. I wanted to hear her voice forever.

I hung up the phone. Uncle Jake was pacing like a lunatic and, dare I say, farting his brains out. "I'm losing my mind," he said. He hurried over to the closet and got out his baseball equipment. "I've got to do something to take my mind off this. Come, Josh, let's play a little baseball."

I smiled at him. He was right; we needed a distraction. I would have done anything to pass the time until they could harvest my bone marrow and make Rocky healthy once again.

CHAPTER TWENTY-FOUR

The sky was growing dark by the time we got to the playground. The overhead lights were already on. Uncle Jake and I stood at home plate. I picked up the bat. Uncle Jake was staring at his mitt, pounding the ball into the pocket.

"Remember how Jones swung the bat the other day?"

"Sure, Uncle Jake."

"Well, you do the same," he said, never once looking up. "Just relax and meet the ball. That's all you have to do."

Uncle Jake turned and walked to the mound. "Okay, get ready, Josh. Here it comes." He started to go into his windup, but then stopped. "Joshua the savior," he called out. "Anyone as special as you can hit a stupid baseball, no?"

I smiled, and Uncle Jake went back into his windup. I saw the ball like I had never seen it before. Against the contrast of the darkening sky, the white baseball stood out like a beacon. I pointed at it with my bat and wasn't thinking about hitting the ball when I swung. I was thinking about Rocky. I saw her stand up and get out of the hospital bed, strong and healthy, with her confident green eyes flashing like lightning during a summer storm. And then I heard the thunder. Uncle Jake spun at the crack of the bat to watch the baseball as it cruised into the night and over the fence.

He threw his mitt on the ground and raced toward home plate. I thought that he was going to stop and shake my hand, but he just scooped me up in his arms and put me over his shoulder.

"Hey, put me down," I said. The truth was I didn't want him to put me down. "You'll hurt yourself lifting a *groyser shtarker* like me."

I heard Uncle Jake erupt in laughter, but he never put me down. He just kept laughing.

And I did too.

CHAPTER TWENTY-FIVE

The conference with Rocky's doctor took place at 11:00 a.m.

The doctor was a stonehearted man named Kimble. I didn't like him. He was cold and seemed to be very impressed with himself. I didn't want him to be Rocky's doctor. I wanted her doctor to be someone warm and fatherly, like Dr. Roosenfeld, my pediatrician from back home. It seemed as if it was an effort for him to explain everything. He never once looked at me. It was as if I was a vial of serum, sitting on a shelf, and that I served no other purpose.

"And so," he said, "the healthy cells will then be injected into your daughter's bloodstream, Rabbi."

"And that's it?" the rabbi asked.

"Yes, that's it," Kimble replied. "The healthy blood cells will find their own way to your daughter's bone marrow."

"Excuse me," Uncle Jake said. "Can we go back to the part about harvesting the marrow?"

"If we need to," Kimble said, as he played with his desk blotter.

"So you stick a needle into my nephew. This is painful, no?"

"Yes," Kimble replied coolly. "Unfortunately, the pelvic region is crammed full of nerve endings. We'll administer analgesics for the pain."

My mind was already made up. The rabbi had already told us that Rocky was having a terrible time with the new treatment. I was not going to turn back.

The door behind me opened unexpectedly.

"Josh?" I recognized my mother's voice. Her arms were around me as soon as I turned around.

"Mom? What are you doing here? You're supposed to be in—"

"We had to come home. We couldn't stand it anymore," she said, kissing me in an embarrassing fashion in front of Uncle Jake, the rabbi and his wife, and Dr. Shithead.

My dad was hovering over me. "How's my little hero?" he said. My mom stepped out of the way so that he could greet me.

"Dad," I said excitedly. I hugged him and was thrilled that they were both here to witness the miracle.

Uncle Jake stood and greeted them. He then introduced them to everyone else. "How did you find us?" Uncle Jake asked.

"We flew in this morning," my dad said. "We went to your apartment. No one was home so we called the hospital and found out that the rabbi had this meeting scheduled."

"It's a wonderful thing your son is doing," the rabbi said to my parents. "You should be very proud of your boy. You raised him well, Robert."

"He's an angel," Esther said. "A sweet angel."

Dr. Kimble yawned. "Will anyone else be coming?"

Uncle Jake glared at him, grumbling something in Yiddish.

My mom said, "Thank you." She looked at my dad, and I knew something was wrong. *"Robert,"* she said to my father, not Bob but Robert, calling him by his formal name as she did whenever the matter was serious.

My dad looked unhappy. He cleared his throat and then looked at the rabbi and his wife. "Rabbi, I've known you since I was a boy, so this is very difficult for me." He paused, and I could see that he was struggling. "My wife and I know how important this is to you, but our Josh is just as important to us."

I saw Esther's mouth curl downward.

"No," the rabbi said. "Don't say this." He already knew what was coming.

My father continued. "We did a little research, and we understand that this procedure is very painful for the donor and not without risk."

"No, Dad, I want to do this," I said in a pleading voice. "It's Rocky's only chance."

The rabbi stood. "Please. Please don't—"

My dad put his hands on my shoulders. "Surely there's something else you can do?" He looked at the doctor, hoping to hear an alternative.

"Frankly, there's not," the doctor replied. "Rachel's had a terrible time with two different types of chemotherapy. A bone marrow transplant is our only viable option."

"Is there any guarantee this will work?" my mom asked.

"We don't offer guarantees, Ma'am. This is a relatively new procedure."

"I'm sorry," my mom said, "You want my son to participate in a painful *experiment*? No. Absolutely not." She sounded outraged. Her head snapped in Uncle Jake's direction. "This is how you take care of our son? How dare you?"

"But, but—" Uncle Jake was helpless before my mother's cutting stare.

"Mom, I'm doing it," I yelled. "You can't stop me."

Dr. Shithead piped up again, "Can we keep our voices down please?" He raised his eyebrows, making it clear that he was irritated.

"Josh, this isn't like asking for a new bike," my dad said. "You just can't—"

"I'm thirteen now," I bellowed. "I'm a man, a bar mitzvah, and I've made up my mind."

My dad smiled sympathetically. He spoke in a firm voice, "Josh, yes, you're a man in the Jewish religion, but you're still a minor . . . and you're still our son."

"May I interrupt?" the rabbi said in a whisper. His voice was subtle, but it commanded attention. Everyone turned to him, waiting for him to speak. "If I can just take you to see my Rachel, if you'll give me one minute of your time." The rabbi's head dropped. "Just look at my suffering child, and if as a parent, you can turn away . . . well, then I won't bother you anymore."

My parents looked at each other. I could see my mom misting over. She opened her purse and took out a tissue. "What do you think, Bob?" she asked.

My dad leaned forward and whispered in her ear, and then she whispered something back to him.

"We're happy to accommodate you, Rabbi, but we're making no promises," he said.

"I understand," the rabbi said. "This is all I can ask."

Dr. Kimble stood and squeezed through the crowd, forcing his way toward the door. "Page me when you've made your decision." He hustled out the door and disappeared.

~~~

We stood at the doorway as the rabbi escorted my mom and dad into Rocky's room. The other girl who had shared the room was gone. Her bed was empty and the privacy curtain had been pulled back. I prayed that she had gotten better.

Rocky was sleeping, wheezing a little with every breath. Her hair was even thinner than the last time I had seen her. A small bald spot was visible.

My dad put his arm around my mom as they watched Rocky sleep. They stood there for moments without saying a word, and I knew in my heart that they ached for her as I did.

Rocky's face was gaunt, her skin stretched tightly over her cheekbones. I turned away. Uncle Jake put his arms around me, clutching me to his chest.

I could hear the rabbi's beseeching voice as he spoke to my parents with words that came from his heart. "In the Talmud, it is written, *He who saves one life, it is as if he had saved the entire world.* This is my daughter, Rachel. This is my entire world."

I heard my mother weeping. A moment later, Uncle Jake stroked my hair and whispered in my ear. "They said yes, Joshua. They said yes."

CHAPTER TWENTY-SIX

I went home with Uncle Jake that night, but it was for the last time. My parents had taken a suite at The Plaza, and I was to return in the morning with my suitcases packed.

I was all wound up and couldn't sleep that night. I wasn't afraid of the procedure, but the sequence of events that would lead to Rocky's recovery kept playing over and over in my mind. I could see the needle being withdrawn from my back and the healthy cells being injected into Rocky. In the next instant, she was standing and smiling. Then the sequence repeated itself and repeated itself again.

It must have been around 2:00 a.m. when I heard Uncle Jake in the bathroom. Sleeping was hopeless, so I got up to talk to him. I had experienced one triumph already that day and was feeling courageous enough to take on one more challenge.

"You're not sleeping? *What's this?*" Uncle Jake asked. "What happened? You always sleep like a log." Uncle Jake looked pretty tired himself, standing in his athletic shirt and boxers in the middle of the apartment. "I'm sorry if I woke you, Josh." The cloud of fart gas surrounding him was so thick you could cut it with a knife.

"I couldn't sleep."

"Oh?" Uncle Jake took a long look at me. "You need to talk? Come into the kitchen; we'll have some milk and cookies."

I followed Uncle Jake into the kitchen. He quickly put milk and two glasses on the table. I went to the cupboard and grabbed the *Oreos*.

"How long have you been getting cancer treatments?" I asked.

"What are you talking about? You're sleepwalking. Go back to bed." His defensive tone told me that I was right.

"I know what's going on."

Uncle Jake sank back into his chair. He didn't protest. He just listened.

"You knew your way around the hospital pretty well. You thought Rachel was going to be on the fourth floor where they do the chemotherapy. Your skin and Rachel's are almost exactly the same color. You rush to the bathroom after every meal and—"

"There's more?"

"Yes. You had a lot more hair the last time you came out to visit us."

Uncle Jake pursed his lips and nodded. "You're quite a detective."

"That's why the rabbi said they couldn't test your blood, isn't it?"

I suppose he could have become obstinate and denied the whole thing, and I almost expected a reaction like that, but he just sat quietly and reflected for a moment before nodding reluctantly. "I had colon surgery in April. They got it all out, but they're giving me a small dose of chemotherapy just to play it safe. It's nothing like what's going on with your Rachel."

"Swear it. Swear you're all right." I was once again fighting back tears.

"Yes, Joshua, I swear."

I jumped out of my chair and into his arms, hugging him, aching in my heart. "Say it again," I demanded.

"I swear, Joshua. I swear. I swear."

CHAPTER TWENTY-SEVEN

Joe Simon caught me leaving the building with my suitcases. I hadn't been avoiding him, but I hadn't been looking for him either.

"You're leaving?" He was wearing the same uniform he had worn every time I had seen him. "But I thought—"

"My parents decided to meet me in New York so that we could fly home together. We're staying in the city a few days before we go."

"I'm gonna miss you, man," he said, and then he did what I never expected him to: he put his arms around me and gave me a hug that almost crushed me. "The whole neighborhood knows what you're doing for the rabbi's daughter. I wish someone cared about me that much. That's pretty cool,

saving someone's life like that and all."
Then he became his usual ghoulish self
again. "How big's the needle they're going to
stick you with?" he asked with intense
interest and a gleeful smile. I told you, he
was weird.

The thought made me shudder. "I
haven't got a clue."

"Oh. Think you're ever coming back?"

"I'd like to . . . I don't know."

"Well God speed, man." He saluted me
like a Roman soldier, smacking his chest
with a closed fist. "Fight the good fight." His
head dropped, and he shuffled off down the
block, disappearing in the direction of his
basement lair to smoke something, I guess,
or build another bomb. I hoped his parents
got their lives together and saw him for the
good soul he was. I hoped they saw it before
it was too late. It was a fight I could not
participate in and an outcome I would never
know.

CHAPTER TWENTY-EIGHT

The rabbi fired Dr. Kimble and replaced him with a doctor named Scheinbloom, a nice Jewish doctor, with curly hair and a sweet bedside manner.

They harvested my bone marrow and performed whatever kind of hocus pocus was necessary in order to introduce my healthy cells into Rocky's body. My lower back hurt like hell for several days. They gave me all kinds of medicine for the pain, but nothing really helped.

I watched over Rocky—at first, minute-by-minute, then hour-by-hour, finally day-by-day. Then that dreaded day came when I had to go home.

Rocky was getting better each day, not because the cancer had gone into remission, but because the chemotherapy had stopped. At first, the number of unhealthy blood cells in her blood count slowly continued to rise. Dr. Scheinbloom said it was to be expected, but it certainly wasn't the kind of miraculous recovery I had hoped for.

I waited and waited to hear the news that Rocky had been cured.

The Mets won the World Series that fall.

Thanksgiving passed, New Year's too.

Somehow almost a year came and went.

Rocky and I talked all the time. At first, I would ask her about her most recent blood test results as soon as we got on the phone, but although the number of unhealthy cells stopped increasing, it never went down. I eventually got smart enough to stop asking her about her blood count because I didn't want to bring down her spirits. We found lots of other things to talk about and discovered that we really did get along.

I was sitting in the den on a Sunday in June, studying for a biology exam—an exam I was destined to fail—when the doorbell rang. My dad, who was just a few feet from the door, stood there looking at me like the cat that had just eaten the canary.

"What's going on?" I asked. His silly grin coaxed a big smile from me. My dad shrugged. I read between the lines, got up, and answered the door myself.

Uncle Jake was standing at the threshold, clutching his throat, pretending to be choking, and yelling, "The smog, I can't breathe. The smog is killing me." He finally stopped play-acting and laughed.

I didn't know whether to laugh or cry. I did neither. I threw my arms around him and hugged him, just shy of popping a few ribs.

"You've grown," he said as he stepped back to look me over.

"Maybe a little."

"Who's talking about your height?" He grinned happily, extended his hand, and examined my chin. "I see you've got whiskers. You're shaving?"

I nodded. "A little."

"Good. *Now you're a man.*" He continued to look me over for a minute and then said, "Please, I left a bag in the taxi. Can you help out an old man?"

"Sure," I said as I walked to the taxi, walking forward, looking backward, happy as a lark. "How long are you staying?" I asked him.

I heard his voice trailing off as he stepped into the house. "Until the Dodgers go back to Brooklyn."

And then I bumped into her. *"Rocky?"* My mouth dropped and hung open. I couldn't speak. She was the Rocky of old: solid, beautiful, eyes like emeralds, and a smile that stole my breath.

"Don't just stand there, surfer boy. Give me a hug."

LAWRENCE KELTER

I did.

Rocky stayed for the summer and with each day that passed, it became more clear that those precious moments we had shared the previous summer were not unique, they were only a beginning, and that we meant more to each other than we could have ever possibly imagined.

We were together when *Love Story* came out that year. Everyone rushed to see it, but we couldn't find the guts to go. We would walk by the theater, night after night, clutching one another. Rocky would look deeply into my eyes, hoping that together we would somehow put together enough courage to walk into the theatre, but we never found the strength. After all, I was not Joshua the savior; I was only Joshua Stern. I was of flesh and blood like anyone else. I had fears and worries, and the heartbreak of *Love Story* was and would always remain a vivid reminder of the tragedy that almost happened to us.

~~~

I have a son of my own now, Jacob, named after his great uncle. Every once in a while I tell him about the summer I spent in Brooklyn in 1969. I tell him about the Mets championship season and how Uncle Jake taught me how to hit a baseball. I also tell him about the Friday afternoon trips to Al's barbershop. To this day, I still enjoy a barbershop shave and getting wrapped up in a hot towel. I even tell him a highly amended version of the rocket-powered glider story . . . but the poignant details, the ones about his mother and me, I keep to myself.

And in that season of faith, Rocky taught me what it meant to be a man. I somehow managed to make her feel like a woman, and we devoted the rest of our lives to each other.

GLOSSARY OF YIDDISH TERMS

Alter kaker – An old fart.

Bupkis – Something of little value, to know little or nothing

Chiam Yankel – A bumpkin

Farklempt – Emotional

Farshtinkener – Rotten, as in a rotten person

Ganse mishpacha – Everyone, the whole clan, extended family

Gonif – A thief

Goonisht – Zero, nothing

Groyse shtarker – A big strong person

Haftarah – A reading from the Jewish bible, part of the bar mitzvah ceremony

Kenahora – A gesture to ward off the evil eye

Kiddush – Refreshments served at a Synagogue

Kishke – Stuffed intestines

Mazel – Luck

Mensch – A good person

Mitzvah – A good deed

Moatse – A prayer said before eating, or drinking wine

Nish do gedachet – It should happen to you!

Oy vey – An expression of dismay or exasperation

Pisher – Someone young or wet behind the ears

Platz – Being so happy you could burst

Putz – A fool, an easy mark

Schmaltz – Chicken fat

Seychel – Common sense

Shainera menchen haut me gelicht in drert – They buried nicer looking people than that.

Shande – A shame, a scandal

Sheyne meydele – Sweet girl

Schlemiel – A dummy, a born loser

Shmear – To spread as in "shmear" cream cheese on a bagel

Shpilkes – Nervous energy, ants in the pants

Shtup – To screw as in sexual intercourse

Shul – A Jewish house of worship, a temple

Tallit – A Jewish prayer shawl

Tsuris – Trouble or woe

Yarmulkes – Traditional Jewish cap

Yente – A busybody

Zhlub – An ill-mannered person, a clumsy oaf

NY Times best-selling novelist Nelson DeMille has actually assisted Kelter in the editing of his early work, and has said, "Lawrence Kelter is an exciting novelist, who reminds me of an early Robert Ludlum."

There are a total of five books in the Stephanie Chalice Thriller series, which include Don't Close Your Eyes, Ransom Beach, The Brain Vault, Our Honored Dead, and Baby Girl Doe. The Series has sold hundreds of thousands of copies worldwide and topped bestseller list in the US and UK.

He is originally from Brooklyn, NY and has not gotten very far from his roots. He currently resides on Long Island with his wife.

His novels are quickly paced and routinely feature a twist ending. For more information, please visit the author at: lawrencekelter.com.

28239555R00104

Made in the USA
Charleston, SC
03 April 2014